JUDGMENT FIRE

TEMPE CRABTREE
MYSTERY SERIES

Novels by Marilyn Meredith
Published by Mundania Press

Tempe Crabtree Mystery Series

Calling the Dead

Judgment Fire

Kindred Spirits

Dispel the Mist

MARILYN MEREDITH

JUDGMENT
FIRE

TEMPE CRABTREE
MYSTERY SERIES

Mundania Press

A Mundania Press Production
Mundania Press LLC
6470A Glenway Avenue, #109
Cincinnati, Ohio 45211-5222

To order additional copies of this book, contact:
books@mundania.com
www.mundania.com

Cover Art © 2007 by Anna Winson
Book Design, Production, and Layout by Daniel J. Reitz, Sr.
Marketing and Promotion by Bob Sanders
Edited by Heather Bollinger

Trade Paperback ISBN: 978-1-59426-484-9
eBook ISBN: 978-1-59426-483-2

First Edition • July 2007
Second Edition • November 2007

Production by Mundania Press LLC
Printed in the United States of America
10 9 8 7 6 5 4 3 2 1

CHAPTER 1

The massive rock barrier of the southern Sierra and its jagged snow-covered pinnacles never failed to inspire Tempe. Normally, the pine, aspen and cedar forest bordering the winding highway calmed and reassured her—until this afternoon.

A face popped into her mind. Someone she hadn't seen or thought of for quite awhile, which added to the apprehension she couldn't shake. Deputy Tempe Crabtree attributed her uneasiness to the fact that her assigned beat, the tiny community of Bear Creek and the surrounding area, would soon be swollen with Memorial Day weekend tourists. Fishermen, swimmers, and water skiers would swarm the banks of Lake Dennison, and visitors in all sorts of vehicles would soon clog the two-lane road to the high country and its many camping sites. Her work load would increase a hundred-fold.

She made a quick pass through Bear Creek and continued upward into the mountains. Her vehicle, a white Blazer with SHERIFF printed in large black letters above the gold county seal on both doors, made her highly visible.

The route followed the river's course and she caught glimpses of it from time to time. Most of the homes and ranches were hidden from view by the thick tangle of wild berry bushes, manzanita, and shadowed woodlands.

Maneuvering the Blazer around a sharp curve, she drew in a quick breath and braked. Fire engulfed the front end of a green mini-van, outlining a person in the front seat. The vehicle was stopped at the side of the road, flames licking at the bordering brush.

Tempe radioed her position and requested assistance before leaping from her vehicle and dashing to the driver's side of the van. She yanked on the handle, but the door wouldn't budge. The cab was filled with smoke. "Get out!"

The driver, a Native American woman in her fifties, faced straight ahead, long fingers gripping the steering wheel. It was Doretha Nightwalker, her silver hair brushed tightly back into a bun. Though Doretha's eyes were open, she didn't seem aware of what was happening.

The windshield and dashboard were melting. Doretha would die if Tempe didn't get her out immediately.

Darting around the van, Tempe leaped the burning brush and reached for the passenger door. After a short struggle, the door opened. "Doretha! You've got to get out now."

The woman didn't react. Tempe scrambled into the front seat. Smoke burned her eyes and the intense heat made breathing difficult. Tempe yanked the woman's arm, but Doretha continued to clutch the steering wheel. Flames sneaked through the cracks of the firewall. One by one, Tempe pried Doretha's fingers loose. Grabbing her around the waist, she yanked the slender woman across the seat and pulled her out of the burning vehicle.

One of the van's tires exploded as Tempe dragged Doretha to her Blazer. Opening the passenger door, she hoisted the woman onto the floor of the Blazer. Doretha stared vacantly.

"Doretha, are you hurt?" Tempe spoke loudly, trying to get through to the woman. Another van tire burst. A siren whined in the distance.

Grasping her wrist, Tempe felt Doretha's pulse. Rapid and strong. No cuts or bruises were on her face. Examining her quickly, Tempe found no obvious broken bones. Of course internal injuries were possible.

The siren grew louder. "We'll have help soon, Doretha."

Doretha still didn't respond.

Tempe grabbed her microphone and contacted the dispatcher. "We've got a single vehicle, fully involved. One victim. We need an ambulance."

Long, slender fingers grabbed Tempe's arm. "No, no ambulance. I'm not hurt." Doretha's voice was deep and raspy.

"You should be checked out by a doctor," Tempe said.

"There's no need."

Tempe shrugged, and picked up the mike. "Cancel the ambulance."

Facing Doretha, Tempe asked, "What happened? Are you sure you're okay?"

"I'm fine. My mind was off somewhere. To tell you the truth, I was thinking about you. All of sudden the car was on fire...I pulled off the road. I don't remember anything after that."

Amazing. "That's strange because you're face popped into my mind just before I turned the corner and discovered your van on fire."

Doretha nodded. "Yes, I thought it was something like that."

Before Tempe could ask what she meant, the fire engine rounded the bend and came to a halt. Captain Roundtree and two volunteers leaped out wearing black-and-yellow turnout gear and helmets and carrying fire extinguishers and hoses. "I don't think they'll be able to save much," Tempe said.

"No, I realize that. A small sacrifice."

"You do have insurance, don't you?"

"Oh, yes. My van will be replaced. But I'm relieved to know that this didn't happen because I was out of harmony. That's when most misfortunes occur."

Doretha, a shaman, viewed the world in a unique manner. Tempe first met her while investigating the disappearance and murder of a small child. Doretha was one of several Native Americans who had recently helped Tempe learn more about her own Yanduchi heritage.

Her curiosity piqued, Tempe asked, "Why do you suppose I had you on my mind just before I came upon you? Something psychic?"

Doretha chuckled. "That's one way of putting it I suppose. However, I think there's a simpler explanation. Our paths were intended to cross."

Why? Did Doretha have a specific reason why they were supposed to see each other? Did the shaman have a problem she needed Tempe's help with? Or was it Tempe who needed Doretha?

Before she could ask any questions, Pete Roundtree walked toward her, pulling off his helmet. His round face, black hair and chestnut skin revealed the Yanduchi ancestry he shared with Doretha and Tempe. Tempe had encouraged Pete to go to school to become a fireman. He, in turn, had assisted Tempe's son Blair to become a volunteer fireman. Blair had been accepted by the state university in San Luis Obispo where he planned to major in fire science. As the son of a highway patrolman killed in the line of duty, Blair received some assistance from the state. Ever since her first husband's death, sixteen year's earlier, Tempe had been saving for Blair's education. If more was needed, Hutch, whom she'd married a short time ago, promised to help.

"This van belongs to you, Miss Nightwalker?" Pete asked.

Apparently not as upset or sad as Tempe suspected she would be under the circumstances, Doretha smiled. "Yes, Captain Roundtree, and I've only had it two weeks. That's what I get for trading in my perfectly good old car."

"Fire's out, but I'm afraid your van isn't worth much now. Any idea what started the fire?" Pete scratched behind one of his large ears.

"I'm afraid not."

He turned his attention toward Tempe. "Have you called a tow truck?"

"No, but I'll do that now unless you have other plans, Doretha."

"That sounds sensible to me though I'm not sure how I'll get home."

"Don't worry, I'll take you," Tempe said.

❧❧

After instructing the truck driver as to where the burned-out hulk should be taken, Tempe headed back toward Bear Creek with Doretha in the passenger seat. She hoped the Yanduchi woman would talk more about what she'd hinted at earlier.

Before she could bring up the subject, Tempe's radio crackled with a domestic disturbance call. Jotting the address on her clipboard, she said, "I'm sorry, Doretha, I won't be able to take you home after all. I'll drop you in town so you can call someone from there."

"I wouldn't mind going with you," Doretha said. "Perhaps I could be of some help."

"I'm sure you could, but I can't do that. Domestic calls can be dangerous."

Doretha didn't argue.

Tempe spotted Hutch's old blue-and-white truck waiting at the intersection of the road leading to Bear Creek Chapel where he served as the pastor. "Look," Tempe pointed out, "There's my husband. I'll signal him. He can take you home."

Frowning, Doretha said, "Oh, I don't know. We didn't hit it very well when we were together last. He might not be eager to do me a favor."

Tempe blinked her lights to get Hutch's attention. "Don't worry, he'll be glad to do it." She parked the Blazer. Hutch was already out of the truck and on his way to meet her, the late afternoon breeze ruffling his thick auburn hair. He wore one of his favorite plaid flannel shirts, faded blue jeans, and cowboy boots.

Doretha climbed out of the passenger side, while Tempe hurried toward her husband.

Greeting her with a quick kiss, he asked, "Hey, Tempe, what's going on?" His gray eyes twinkled with curiosity.

"Remember Doretha Nightwalker?"

Hutch glanced past Tempe at the woman who had almost reached them. "Of course, but what is she doing..."

"She'll have to explain. She can do that while you're taking her home. Got to dash, I'm on a call." Tempe whirled around and jogged back to the Blazer.

She heard Hutch saying, "How are you, Miss Nightwalker?"

Doretha's answer was lost to Tempe, as she sped away.

The address the dispatcher gave Tempe was on the other side of Bear Creek. Tempe recognized it. She'd been there twice before on a family disturbance call.

Passing through the town, she had to slow down because of the Friday night traffic. The only market was busy. Residents and visitors filled the front lot. Bear Creek Inn had a full house too. All the parking spaces in front of The Saloon and The Café across the street were filled. Though she'd turned on her light bar, she didn't run the siren. A young mother holding a toddler by the hand and a sack of groceries in the other, flashed her a smile while scurrying across the road.

Once she reached the outskirts of town, Tempe sped up. Little traffic was in front of her, all of it was heading the other way—toward Bear Creek: commuters returning home, visitors to the Inn and other tourist attractions higher in the mountains. Folks were already anticipating the coming holiday.

Making a right-hand turn on Aspen Road, Tempe began thinking about the couple she would soon encounter. The husband, Tom Cannata, was a respected leader of the Bear Creek community and a building contractor with plenty of work. Jackie, his wife, belonged to all the women's clubs. Her son from a previous marriage was the same age as Blair.

The first time Tempe dealt with the Cannatas' problems was about four year's ago, not long after their marriage. They were partying with several other couples on a houseboat in the middle of the lake. Lucky for Jackie, Tempe had been cruising the lake's parking lot after being attracted by angry shouts and screams coming from the boat. The colored lights decorating the roof reflected gaily in the black water.

She'd driven down to the shore line. No sooner had she parked, when a woman toppled from the houseboat into the lake. The people on the boat hollered and yelled, but no one went in after her—and she didn't come up.

Tempe yanked off her shoes, unfastened her belt and tossed it along with her holster and gun into the front seat of the Blazer and dashed into the water. Swimming hard until she reached the boat, she dived where she'd seen the woman disappear.

The first time down, Tempe found nothing. She came up gasping for air. She had a vague remembrance of a blur of white faces and people shouting at her. Diving again, Tempe pulled hard with her arms, going deeper. It was so dark and murky, she couldn't see anything. She swung around, and her fingers touched what felt like a foot. She yanked, felt a leg and a torso. Circling the body with one arm, she swam upward with her other hand, pulling and kicking herself through the water. When she broke the surface, a cheer went up above her.

Gasping for air, she stared at the victim. Even with her tanned face turned ashen, her bleached hair darkened and plastered to her head, Tempe recognized Jackie Cannata.

Arms reached over the side of the boat. Tempe lifted Jackie upward and someone hauled her aboard. Big hands grabbed Tempe under the arms, lifting her into the boat. Voices were raised all around her.

"Wow. That was brave of you, Deputy."

"My, God, Jackie isn't breathing."

"Someone, do something!'

"Get us into shore."

Jackie lay at Tempe's feet, water pooling around the shapely body clad in a brightly colored bikini. Ignoring everyone, Tempe knelt beside the woman. Her fingers pressed against Jackie's neck, she felt a weak, thready pulse. Pushing her head back and pinching her nose, Tempe blew into Jackie's mouth. She did it again.

Jackie gasped, her body arching. Water spewed out of her mouth and Tempe leaned out of the way. Coughing, and gagging, Jackie vomited. From the smell, much of it was alcohol.

Once it was obvious Jackie would be all right despite her surprise midnight swim, the bruise on her cheek and a cut and swollen lip, Tempe stood. "Now, will someone please tell me what this is all about?"

All eyes turned toward Tom Cannata. He flashed a huge smile at Tempe, "I'm afraid I got carried away, Deputy. You know how it is. We were horsing around and it got out of hand."

Tempe glanced at Jackie. "How about you, Mrs. Cannata. Do you want to tell me what happened to you? How'd you get that split lip?"

Jackie's fingers flew to her lip. She looked surprised. "I guess I must have hit something when I fell out of the boat."

"Fell or were you were pushed?" Tempe suggested.

Without looking at her husband, Jackie said, "Oh, my. It was nothing like that. Just as my husband told you, we were only playing around."

"Anyone else want to tell me what happened?"

Tempe was acquainted with most of the party. If there were such a thing as a social set in Bear Creek, all were present. No one made eye contact with Tempe. Some turned away.

"Too bad. Let's get this boat to shore. Mrs. Cannata should be examined by a doctor."

After that, Tempe had been called to the Cannata home three more times when neighbors reported the sounds of fighting. Jackie explained away her bruises as something she'd done to herself due to clumsiness. Tom, always charming and in control, was the perfect host. Jackie's son, Ronnie Keplinger, had been present during Tempe's questioning on one occasion. Though he said nothing, he'd stood in the hallway, with an unreadable expression, his arms crossed.

The Cannata home was at the end of the Aspen Road, a new, two-story, fashioned after an old-time farm house and set off by a rustic, split-rail fence. The sun had disappeared behind the boulder-studded hills though the sky was still bright. Tempe pulled into the driveway behind Tom's silver BMW. As she climbed from the Blazer, she heard a male voice shouting and a woman screaming. Maybe this time there would be enough evidence of violence to arrest Tom whether Jackie wanted to press charges or not.

As she ran up the circular path, the front door banged open and

Ronnie burst out onto the porch. Tall and gangly, his head was shaved. An Army issue camouflage shirt gaped open over an olive green T-shirt. Baggy camouflage pants were tucked into combat boots. Ronnie must have been in new phase. Last time Tempe had seen him, his hair was dyed purple, pink and green and combed into spikes.

"They're at it again," he snarled, stomping past her.

Tempe pushed through the door he'd left open and stepped into the foyer. The yelling and screaming came from upstairs though it was obvious the fight had been going on downstairs as well. A ceramic lamp lay shattered on the cream colored carpet of the living room. An antique chair had been overturned.

Grabbing the oak banister, Tempe took the stairs two at a time. When she reached the landing, she heard the sound of a hand hitting flesh and Jackie cry out in pain.

Tempe swung open the door that she knew led to master bedroom. "Hey! What's going on here?"

CHAPTER 2

Jackie Cannata lay sprawled across a floral, satin bedspread, her arms folded protectively across her face. Tom leaned over her.

"Mr. Cannata," Tempe said.

At the sound of Tempe's voice he whirled around. His handsome face underwent a quick transformation, from livid and threatening, to surprise. Silver accented his sideburns, contrasting with his otherwise dark brown hair.

He straightened, smoothing his hair, and quickly tucked in his shirt tail. "What are you doing here, Deputy Crabtree?" Once again his expression changed. He grinned, exposing his big teeth, in a failed attempt at friendliness.

"Someone in the neighborhood reported that you and your wife were fighting. Seems they were concerned about her well-being."

The smile disappeared. "Damn nosy neighbors."

Tempe stepped toward the bed even though Tom blocked her view of Jackie. "Mrs. Cannata, do you want to tell me what's going on here?"

A whimper came from behind him.

Tom held up both hands, palms facing Tempe. "Listen, Deputy, it isn't what you think. I got home earlier than usual this evening. Thought Jackie and I could head on up to the Inn for a few drinks and dinner but my dear wife was already half-sloshed. She started an argument about nothing and we got into a shouting match. You know how it is."

"Step aside, Mr. Cannata. Let me look at your wife." Tempe stared directly into Tom's eyes.

He crossed his arms and continued to block Tempe's view of his wife. "She's a real mess. Fell down the stairs. So drunk she can't even stay on her feet."

"Move out of the way."

"Whatever you say, Deputy. But I didn't lay a hand on her. She did it to herself." He shifted slightly giving Tempe access to his wife.

Jackie pulled herself to a sitting position on the edge of the bed, her head lowered, long blonde tresses covering her face. Her shoulders shook as she sniffled.

"Let me look at your face, Mrs. Cannata."

The hands came away slowly and she lifted her head. Blood oozed from a deep cut near her eyebrow and a bruise marred her cheek.

"Oh, sweetheart, I didn't realize you were hurt that..." Tom reached toward her and Jackie cringed.

"I'd like you to step back, Mr. Cannata." Tempe said.

"But..."

"Do it." Tempe said.

"This is my wife and my home," Tom protested, but he moved several feet away.

"Yes, and I'm trying to find out what's going on here." Tempe unhooked her radio from her belt. She needed back-up.

"What are you doing?" Tom asked, as Tempe radioed for help. "That isn't necessary. Jackie and I can work this out without you guys around. Isn't that right, honey?"

Jackie turned her head away, whimpering.

"Why don't I get some ice for that cut?" Tom said, easing toward the door.

Pictures would have to be taken of Jackie's face before she received treatment. But until another deputy arrived, Tempe didn't want to do anything that might trigger Tom to be more violent. She had to keep the situation controlled.

"Why don't we all go downstairs and you can each tell me your side?" she said, forcing herself to smile at Tom. "Maybe you could fix us some coffee."

"Yeah, okay." Tom moved slowly out of the room.

Tempe sat on the bed beside Jackie and hugged her shoulder. "Do you want to tell me what this was all about?"

Jackie sobbed as she gasped out her story. "I only had one drink...sometimes I need it. Usually he's really nice...you know that. Everyone thinks he's charming."

"He wasn't so charming tonight."

In a tiny voice, she said, "Once in awhile he blows up for no reason at all."

"What happened this evening?"

"Oh, it isn't important."

"Yes, it is, Mrs. Cannata. I want you to be honest with me."

She sighed. "I was in the kitchen when he came home. He spotted my Vodka cooler and smelled it. I shouldn't have been drinking by myself. I know how he hates that. It's all my fault."

"No, you're wrong. He had no reason to hit you. Go on."

"He threw the glass at me. He started yelling and cussing." She wiped her nose with her hand.

Tempe pulled a tissue from the box on the table beside the bed and handed it to Jackie.

She blew her nose before continuing. "I screamed back at him. Called him awful names. It's no wonder he got so mad."

"You aren't responsible for his actions. What happened next?"

The rest came out in a big rush. "We yelled at each other some more. He threw me across the floor. I got up and ran into the living room and he came after me. My son, Ronnie, came downstairs and yelled at Tom to leave me alone. Tom threw the lamp at him and told him to get out. Ronnie began hollering at me to leave Tom. Tom went after him with a chair, and I started up the stairs. I thought I could lock myself in the bedroom until he calmed down, but he caught up with me before I could close the door. He socked me. That's when I got this." She winced as she touched the cut near her eyebrow. "When I screamed, he slapped me so hard I fell on the bed. Then you came in."

"I'm going to arrest Tom, but I don't want to do it until another deputy arrives. You need to see a doctor. If I help, can you make it downstairs?"

"I'll be all right," Jackie said, but she winced when she grabbed Tempe's arm to pull herself up. "You don't have to arrest him. He's calmed down now. I'm sure he's sorry. I don't want to bring charges against him."

"It's out of your hands, Mrs. Cannata. I have sufficient evidence of assault to arrest him whether you want it or not."

Jackie clung to Tempe's arm. "Don't do that, Deputy, please. It'll just make matters worse."

"No, Mrs. Cannata, you're wrong. Matters will be worse if he's not stopped. If you want to stay married to him, that's your business. Letting him know he can't keep on hitting you, that's my business.

Spousal abuse is a crime. There are people that can help you get out of this situation."

A loud banging on the front door gave Tempe the signal she needed.

"Come on Mrs. Cannata, time to go downstairs. That's my back-up."

Tom opened the door to Deputy Bradley, pink-cheeked, good-looking and young. His overly-developed muscles strained the seams of his sharply creased uniform. Bradley quickly took in the scene before he glanced upward at Tempe.

Jackie clung to the banister as she slowly descended the stairs, Tempe beside her.

Tom rubbed his palms together. "Well. Let's all go into the dining room, shall we? The coffee's ready."

Leaving Jackie, Tempe hurried down the steps. "Bradley, read Mr. Cannata his rights. He's under arrest for spousal abuse."

"You're kidding, right? My wife and I had a little argument. All husbands and wives fight. You can't arrest me, deputy. What would people think? It'll hurt my business." Tom's head jerked back and forth between Tempe and Deputy Bradley.

"You should have thought of that before you decided to assault your wife," Tempe said. "Put your hands against the wall and spread your legs. Go ahead, Bradley, read him his rights."

While Bradley read from the card he drew from his breast pocket, Tempe patted Tom down, looking for weapons. She didn't find any, hadn't expected to, but it was procedure. While she fastened handcuffs around Tom's wrists he continued protesting loudly.

"I'll have your badge, Deputy. You'll be sorry you ever messed with me." His complexion was close to purple, his eyes narrowed, filled with hate.

Tempe ignored him. She'd been threatened too many times to be concerned. "Take him in for me, Bradley. I have to get pictures and see that Mrs. Cannata's wounds are treated."

"Glad to. Come with me, sir." Bradley grasped Tom's elbow and led him outside.

Tempe heard Tom's protests even after the door was closed. "Hey, fella, you've got to listen to reason..."

Using the camera from her Blazer, Tempe took several shots of Jackie's injuries, the broken lamp and overturned chair. When she'd finished, she said, "Let me drive you to the emergency room."

Jackie shook her head.

"That cut by your eye may need stitches."

"I'll go to Dr. McClatchey's." He was the only physician in the local area. Semi-retired, he opened the office in his home only once a week, though, when necessary, he treated emergency cases.

"Okay. I'll give him a call to make sure he's there." Tempe started for the phone on the table in the foyer.

"There's no need. This is the evening he always sees patients."

"Good. I'll want him to write a report about your injuries. I'll need it for evidence."

Jackie sighed hugely, and Tempe knew she hadn't intended to go to the doctor at all.

"Come on, Mrs. Cannata. Let's get this over with."

As they stepped onto the walkway outside, an over-weight woman hurried toward them, a long floral skirt swirling around sturdy legs. "Oh, my God, Jackie. What on earth happened to you?"

Jackie lowered her head, her blonde curls falling forward to hide the bruise on her cheek. Her hand flew up to shield the cut near her eyebrow. "It's nothing. I'm okay." She walked faster.

The woman sidled closer. "I saw the other deputy taking Tom away. He beat you up, didn't he? I heard you screaming, Jackie. I'm the one who called 911."

Jackie didn't comment.

Tempe held the passenger door of the Blazer open and Jackie climbed in.

After closing the door, Tempe turned to the woman, "Thank you for calling it in. That was the right thing to do."

The woman looked slightly familiar, though Tempe couldn't remember either her name or where they'd met.

"Yvette La Rue." She stuck out a plump, dimpled hand. "I was a year behind you in high school. I don't suppose you remember me." Shoulder-length, dyed red curls framed her round face. Bright green eye-shadow, false lashes, an abundance of pink blush on her puffy cheeks, and red lipstick gave her an almost clown-like appearance. An oversize maroon knobby sweater covered her lumpy torso.

"Not really. Sorry. You'll have to excuse me. I'm in a hurry."

The woman called out after her, "My name was Slader back then."

When Tempe drove away, Jackie said, "I might have known she'd be the one. She'll do anything to get back at me."

"A neighbor?" Tempe asked.

Jackie nodded. "She moved in a couple of months ago. Two houses down. She dislikes me so much I can't imagine why she wanted to live so close."

"If she's been in Bear Creek such a short time, what on earth happened to cause such a problem between the two of you." Tempe wished she could remember Yvette, but nothing came back.

"It's from a long time ago. When we were in high school together. Stupid kid stuff. I don't even remember."

"Maybe she doesn't either. She acted genuinely concerned about you. And she did call 911."

"She did it to embarrass me."

"Oh, come on. Your husband could have injured you more seriously if he hadn't been stopped."

"She doesn't care what happens to me. In fact, she's probably happy to know Tom and I don't get along."

Obviously Tempe couldn't convince Jackie otherwise, but she doubted Yvette had any other motive than to stop the abuse. Jackie was obviously paranoid about her. Tempe wondered where that came from.

Steering the Blazer along the familiar road, she thought about her arrest report and whether she needed more information from Jackie. She drove west on the highway, making a left on the same street that led to the rustic cottage she shared with Hutch and Blair.

Crossing the river, she passed her turnoff and the lane leading to the old cemetery on the hill that held the remains of her pioneer relatives, some of the first people to settle in the Bear Creek area. Of course, her ancestors on the other side of the family, the Yanduchi Indians, had lived here for centuries before that.

McClatcheys' two-story, redwood house loomed ahead. The circular driveway was jammed with vehicles attesting to the fact that the doctor was indeed seeing patients.

Jackie scrunched down in the seat. "Darn. Look how many people are here. If Yvette hasn't already passed the word, everyone in Bear Creek is going to know what happened to me."

"I'll go in first and arrange for you to go directly into the inner office."

For the greater part of the rest of her shift, Tempe saw that Tom was properly booked and wrote her report, filing it, along with the photos and a copy of Dr. McClatchey's medical treatment of Jackie Cannata.

Fortunately, even though it was Friday, the remainder of the evening was quiet. Bear Creek was usually peaceful and the crime rate low. For the most part, her job dealt with traffic violations and an occasional drunk driver. All the citizens knew her, and she knew most of them, at least by sight. Being the resident deputy in Bear Creek was nothing like working in law enforcement in the valley, though sometimes she did have to deal with the worst of human behavior.

The volunteer senior patrol car cruising up and down the highway and through the various neighborhoods also helped keep things calm. Tempe wondered if the fairly new volunteer unit would have a similar effect on the impending crowd of visitors soon to overrun the area she was responsible for.

She returned home soon after midnight. Hutch and Blair were sound asleep. She slid in beside her husband and almost immediately fell asleep.

No emergency calls interrupted her slumber, and she awoke in the morning to the enticing scent and sound of bacon sizzling in the kitchen. She smiled as she climbed out of bed. Hutch was preparing breakfast.

After showering, donning her sweats, and braiding her black hair into a single queue left hanging down her back, Tempe joined Hutch in the kitchen.

He greeted her with a kiss. "You look rested. Did you have a good night?" He studied her face carefully, as he did most mornings, apparently checking to see if her job had left any visible signs.

"Pretty quiet, except for a problem at the Cannata home." Tempe poured herself a cup of coffee. "Where's Blair? Already off to the fire station?"

Hutch grinned, revealing a dimple. "This is Saturday, isn't it? What's wrong with the Cannatas?"

"I had to arrest Tom for spousal abuse." Tempe quickly described what had happened.

"Oh dear. And that isn't his only problem.

CHAPTER 3

"Seems one of Tom's neighbors is mad at him too," Hutch said. "Are you ready for breakfast? There's bacon on and I can fix you a couple of eggs."

"Just bacon and toast. "Tempe dropped two slices of rye bread into the toaster. "I'd like to get in a run this morning. Who was the neighbor, Yvette LaRue? She's the one who made the 911 call. There's bad blood between her and Jackie."

"Nope. It wasn't Mrs. LaRue." He turned a couple of pages of the newspaper. "Here it is."

Tempe buttered her toast while Hutch, tortoise-shell rimmed glasses perched on his freckled nose, auburn hair rumpled, read aloud.

"The headline says, 'NEIGHBORS CLAIM BEAR CREEK POND A THREAT.'" Hutch pulled out a chair and sat opposite Tempe at the round table. "The quotes are from Spencer Gullott. You know him, don't you?"

Gullott, known as Spence around Bear Creek, was a computer programmer who worked out of his home. Tall and lean to the point of gauntness, Spence seemed always to have his mind on something other than what he was doing. Twice Tempe had stopped him for driving too slowly on the highway, apparently unaware that several vehicles were backed up behind him. He'd blinked at her through the thick glasses perched on his sharp nose, apologized profusely and driven off in his old Volvo station wagon at the same slow pace.

"What's his problem?"

Hutch scanned the article. "It seems Tom diverted water from the creek to fill a huge pond on his property."

"Plenty of others have done the same."

"Spence's home is directly below this pond and he's convinced it isn't properly dammed and poses a threat to him and his family."

Tempe nodded. "I can see why he might be worried. That's a lot of water. If the earth dam gave way, the pond would dump it all on top of the Gullotts' house."

"That's Spence's fear."

"Did Tom comment?"

"At length. Gives his qualifications as a contractor, and years of experience. He calls Spence, an egg-headed nincompoop who doesn't know his backside from a hole in the ground."

"Oh, my. I'm sure that didn't set well with Spence." Tempe sipped the coffee. "How did you and Doretha get along yesterday? Did you get her back to the reservation without an argument?"

"No argument, though we did have quite a lively discussion."

Tempe laughed. "I'll bet." Doretha's Native American rituals and teachings conflicted with Hutch's Christian traditions and beliefs.

"She's got a wild notion that you're in some kind of danger. You'd have been proud of me. I told her danger came with your job."

"Good for you."

"Unfortunately, that didn't stop her. She said that what happened to her van was part of the warning she needed to pass along to you. She sounded convinced. So consider yourself warned."

She could tell by Hutch's tone that he didn't think much of Doretha's views—nor did Tempe, really. Maybe if she could make some sense of the warning. "Did she give any indication of what I should be looking out for?"

Hutch rolled his eyes. "Surely you aren't taking this to heart?"

"No, of course not." She didn't plan to seek Doretha out, but if their paths crossed again, she'd certainly ask for an explanation. "I think I'll go for my run now."

❧❧

When she returned, Tempe was surprised that Hutch's old blue-and-white truck was gone from the driveway. Since he hadn't mentioned any appointments this morning, she guessed something came up. The phone rang when she opened the back door.

The voice on the other end was hysterical. At first Tempe didn't recognize Jackie Cannata.

"I told you not to arrest him. He called me from jail this morning. He says he's going to kill me as soon as he gets out. Deputy Crabtree, this is all your fault! What am I going to do?" She ended with a wail.

"You don't have to do anything, Mrs. Cannata. Your husband isn't going to lay a hand on you. He's going to stay in jail at least until Monday."

"But then what? He'll come after me, I just know it."

"Don't worry, Jackie, I doubt he's that stupid." But Tempe did wonder about the man's judgment. It certainly wasn't smart to be making threatening calls from the sub-station.

As she suggested that Jackie get a restraining order against Tom, she noticed a note propped against the sugar bowl.

"Franklin Brody's wife in car wreck. Going to Dennison Hospital to be with them. Love, Hutch."

Her husband was called away from home nearly as much as she. Tempe jerked her attention back to Jackie. "Listen, Mrs. Cannata, maybe you shouldn't be alone. Isn't there someone you could stay with for a few days?"

"I can't go away. I have to be here for Ronnie."

Like Tempe's son, Blair, Ronnie was eighteen, or close to it. "Oh, I bet he can take care of himself." Tempe thought he'd probably love the chance to stay in the house alone.

Jackie lowered her voice. "That's not the problem. I don't dare leave Ronnie here unsupervised. There's no telling what he might do."

Tempe didn't remember Jackie having that much concern for her son in the past. While the boy was in his early teens, he roamed Bear Creek at all hours. She once caught him smoking pot in the park. "All I can do is make suggestions, any action is up to you."

After rambling on a few more minutes, Jackie seemed to run out of breath. Tempe closed the conversation. "If you have another emergency, call 911. Someone will get to you right away."

The door banged open and Blair dashed in. "Hi, Mom. Came home to eat." He leaned down to kiss her on the cheek. His cornsilk hair was swept back from his face in a style favored by young men in popular magazine ads.

"I made tuna sandwiches. What's going on in town?"

"Not much. Did you hear about Mrs. Brody?" Blair straddled a chair and began munching on a sandwich.

Tempe poured him a glass of milk. "Just that she's been in an accident. That's where Hutch is now, at the hospital with her and Frank."

"It was a bad one. Critical injuries. Had to use the jaws to get her out."

"Oh, dear."

Blair began eating his second sandwich when Tempe asked, "Do you ever see Ronnie Keplinger anymore?"

Frowning, Blair said, "Ronnie and I haven't been friends since second grade. What about him?"

"Just wondered. His mother and step-father are having problems. I thought he might have said something to you."

"He didn't, but everyone else in town is gossiping about Mr. Cannata punching his wife. They say you arrested him."

"That's true."

"Hey, good for you." Blair gulped down the rest of his milk and stood. "Gotta get back to the station. By the way, Ronnie doesn't like his step-father much."

Fortunately, after some minor rough moments at the beginning of her marriage, Blair now seemed genuinely fond of his step-father, Hutch.

"How do you know that?"

"He told me before he dropped out of school."

"Ronnie doesn't go to school anymore?"

"Quit the day he turned eighteen. He'd always said he was going to do that. I'm surprised he stayed as long as he did. He's pretty weird, you know."

She did. With his shaved head and Army clothing, he looked like he might be involved with either a racist or survivalist group.

"He's not real crazy about his mother either."

"Oh?"

"He never said anything good about her before she remarried, and when she did, he began calling her terrible names."

"Since you don't hang with him, how do you know all this?"

"With Ronnie, it's not hard to know how he feels about everything. He always talks so loud you can't help but hear if you're anywhere around."

Blair changed the subject to his plans after graduation. Everything was geared toward his eventually working as a firefighter. His ambitions were obvious to everyone who knew him. From the time he turned sixteen, he hung around the fire station, doing chores and taking the training. He even went on calls long before he was old enough to be officially sworn in as a volunteer.

After Blair left to return to the fire station, Tempe put in a load of laundry.

Hutch called to report on Clare Brody. Her injuries were extensive and she was still in the operating room. He finished with, "I'm going to stay with Frank until the surgery is over. When I can leave, I'll go straight to the chapel to finish my sermon. Pray for Clare and Frank."

She didn't see either Hutch or Blair before she left for work, nor was Hutch home when she took her dinner break. Once again, her shift was exceptionally calm for a Saturday night. She feared everyone was saving up all their antics for the big weekend.

Tempe had plenty of time to think as she drove around and she considered her encounter with Doretha. The shaman said their paths were intended to cross but didn't have the time or inclination to explain why. Hutch mentioned that Doretha had warned of some danger ahead for Tempe. Maybe if she had time, she'd visit Doretha and see if she might expound a bit on her theory.

When Tempe made one last pass through town, the red glow from a cigarette attracted her attention to a lone figure sitting on a picnic table in the park. The silhouettes of the slide, swing-set and merry-go-round loomed like mechanical monsters in the dark background.

She parked the Blazer and strode toward the person. As she drew closer, she recognized Ronnie Keplinger. He sucked again on the cigarette and blew out a thick stream of smoke, making no effort to hide the can of beer he held in his hand. He was dressed as usual in camouflage Army fatigues and combat boots.

"Yo, Deputy. What's happening?"

"What're you doing out here, Ronnie?"

"What's it look like?"

"You're breaking a couple of laws, Ronnie. You're not old enough to be drinking and this is a public place."

"So what're you gonna do? Haul me in?"

"Probably not. But maybe we should talk. Why don't you give me the beer?"

"What's the matter? Can't afford to buy your own?" He took a long drink and crushed the can with one hand before passing it to Tempe.

She tossed it into the nearby trash can.

"Good shot."

"You ought to be home with your mother," Tempe said.

"Ha! Why would I want to do that?"

"She's just gone through a traumatic experience, Ronnie. She needs your support."

"Oh, yeah, what was that?"

"Being assaulted by her husband."

"That's nothing new. Goes on all the time. Anyway, she asks for it."

Tempe felt anger. "No one asks to be beaten, Ronnie."

"No, I guess not. I sure didn't, but that didn't keep Mom from doing it to me when I was too little to get away from her." Though his face didn't lose its usual sullen expression, his voice quavered slightly. For an instant she saw the sweet, timid, eight year-old Ronnie who had come to Blair's birthday party so long ago. She never suspected Jackie beat her son. At that time, Tempe was still a fairly new deputy, working in other parts of Tulare County, and didn't have much contact with the residents of Bear Creek.

"That was wrong, of course. But it's also wrong for a man to strike his wife. Domestic violence is a crime just like any other."

"Yeah, yeah."

"Your mother does need you, Ronnie. She's scared and worried about what will happen when Tom gets out of jail."

Ronnie pulled a pack of cigarettes from his shirt pocket. Plucking one out, he growled, "Hey, I warned her not to marry that hard-ass. I told her the smooth way he acted when he was sniffing around her was all a big put-on, but she wouldn't believe me. Besides, what goes around, comes around. She's getting hers now. Can't say I'm broken up about it."

"She's your mother," Tempe said, though she realized any argument was probably futile.

"She gave birth to me, anyway." He struck a match on the rough surface of the table top, held the flame to the cigarette, and inhaled. "But she doesn't like me, and I sure as hell don't like her. Tom can kill her for all I care."

"Oh, Ronnie, you don't mean that."

"Yeah, I do. Thought about doing it myself a few times."

She decided to ignore his comment. "What are your plans for tonight?"

"Oh, I was gonna head back to the house pretty soon. By the time I get there, Mom will be in bed. Saves a lot of hassles that way."

"What if I take you home?"

"Now?" Ronnie glanced at a military watch on his wrist. "Yeah, okay. I guess it's late enough."

On the way to Aspen Road, Tempe asked, "What do you plan to do with your life, Ronnie?"

"What do you care?" he snapped, staring out the side window.

"I really am interested. After all, I've known you since you were a little boy. Have you thought about continuing your education?"

"I hate school."

"Too bad. Blair's going to college in San Luis Obispo. He wants to be a fire fighter."

"Big deal."

"Surely you have some dreams...something you'd like to do."

"Maybe go in the Army and shoot people. There's always a war going on somewhere."

She knew he was trying to shock her. "Have you talked to a recruiter yet?"

"Of course," he growled. "Gotta have a diploma."

"That's not impossible, you know. Why don't you try for a GED?"

"Ha! Probably couldn't pass the test."

Tempe explained about the classes at the adult school designed to help students pass the GED test. "You could do that."

"I suppose."

"Think about it, Ronnie. If you really want to go in the Army, wouldn't it be worth it? Anything you really want is worth working for, isn't it? Don't waste your life."

She'd finished her plea and pulled into the Cannatas' driveway at the same time. Turning to Ronnie, she was surprised to see his lower lip quiver as though he might be going to cry. Perhaps she'd actually gotten through to him.

Instead of crying, he exploded in laughter.

CHAPTER 4

Though Monday was supposed to be one of Tempe's days off, when she and Hutch were finishing breakfast, Sergeant Guthrie called her at home. He asked her to report to his office.

"What's going on?" Hutch asked as she hung up the phone.

She sighed. "That was the Sergeant. I have to go in."

"Why?"

"He didn't say. Could be about Tom Cannata. He'll probably get out on bail today."

"I was hoping you could go with me to visit Clare. She's still in ICU, but she's doing pretty well, considering."

"The prayers must be working."

"Crabtree, sit down," the Sergeant greeted when Tempe entered his tiny, crowded office. He sat behind a metal desk that took up most of the space. Behind him, a bookcase was crammed with books, folders, and notebooks. Posters, curled announcements, and jokes cut from law-enforcement magazines were taped to the drab, gray walls.

She perched on the edge of one of two folding chairs. "What's going on, Sergeant?"

"Wanted to talk about the wife beater." He shuffled through a stack of papers until he came to a folder containing what Tempe recognized as her report on Tom Cannata.

"What do you want to know?"

Guthrie leaned back, cradling his thick neck with his meaty hands. His military cut, salt-and-pepper hair emphasized the roundness of his head. "What's the potential for this man doing his wife more harm?"

Tempe shrugged. "Who knows? There's always that possibility. Mrs. Cannata told me that he called her from jail, making threats."

"He's probably on his way home as I speak. We've been getting some pressure about him from influential places. He didn't have any problem making bail."

"You have something in mind for me to do?" Tempe asked, though she knew the answer.

A smile flickered briefly on Guthrie's ruddy face. He leaned toward her, his small eyes bright beneath shaggy brows. "I know this is your day off, but I want you to keep an eye on the Cannatas. Defuse any situation that might be brewing."

"Exactly what are you asking, Sergeant? Do you want me to go there now? Am I supposed to work a regular shift? Will I get overtime?"

"Tell you what, Crabtree, much as I hate to authorize overtime, I will in this instance. Why don't you to play it by ear. Drop by the house, check out what's going on."

Tempe was grateful the Sergeant recognized the potential for disaster in the Cannatas' marital situation.

Before she could comment the Sergeant continued, "Use your women's intuition on this one. Or some of that Indian mumbo jumbo. Whatever it takes."

Tempe winced. She stood, turning away to hide her displeasure. It was just like him to put her down because she was a woman and part Native American.

⁓⁓

Tom Cannata was climbing into his silver BMW when Tempe arrived. Her heartbeat quickened, but she was relieved to see Jackie standing on the porch.

"Hold up a minute, Mr. Cannata," she called, getting out of the Blazer. "I'd like to talk to you."

"Haven't you done enough to me already?" he growled from where he stood beside the open door of his car.

"You did it to yourself, sir," Tempe said as she approached the visibly angry man.

"What do you want? I'm in a hurry."

"I want to make sure there's no repetition of what happened here the other night."

"You don't have to worry about that, Deputy. I'm out of the house and this marriage."

"It doesn't have to be that way, you know. You two could get counseling..."

"Forget it, I'm not interested." He glowered at her. "I'm on my way to Fresno. I have a meeting and I'm late already." He slid into the black leather driver's seat and slammed the door.

Tempe watched as he backed out of the driveway.

"Good riddance," Jackie called out.

"Do you have a few minutes?" Tempe asked.

"Sure. I'm not going anywhere looking like this. The bastard." Though Jackie had combed her blonde hair over her forehead to hide the stitches, the make-up on her cheek didn't completely conceal the bluish tinge of the bruise. "Come on in."

She led Tempe into a large, airy kitchen. White cabinets and a refrigerator with glass fronts exposed neatly arranged shelves of food and dishes. Copper bottom pots hung from a circular rack suspended from the ceiling. Towels and pottery accessories matched the dark blue counter. "Coffee?"

"Sure." Tempe took a seat at the white kitchen table.

Jackie brought a cup of coffee to her.

"Thanks," Tempe said. "Did you get a restraining order?"

"No. But it doesn't matter, does it? He says he's getting a divorce."

"It would still be a good idea. I'll go with you, if you like."

"No, that's not necessary. Maybe I'll take care of it later."

"Okay, but I hope you'll give it some serious thought." Tempe knew Jackie had no intention of getting a restraining order. After taking a sip of the fragrant brew, Tempe asked, "Where is Tom off to now?"

"Some kind of out-of-town business meeting. He packed a suitcase, I suppose he's staying overnight. During the best times he never gave me any details about his work. I'm sorry, do you want cream or sugar?"

"No thanks."

Jackie sat opposite her. Though apparently the situation had calmed somewhat, Tempe still didn't feel comfortable. "Do you folks keep guns?" Nearly everyone in Bear Creek owned guns.

Jackie blinked several times and stared beyond Tempe. "We've got a rifle. Doesn't everyone? Need something to kill rattlesnakes...and I certainly know one."

Tempe ignored her comment. "That's all? Neither you or Tom has a handgun?"

By the expression on Jackie's face, Tempe guessed both of them did. But Jackie shook her head.

Tempe sipped her coffee and studied Jackie as she squirmed in her seat and fluffed her blonde tresses. Finally she stood, striding across the shiny white-and-blue floor tiles.

"Tell me, do you think Tom will be back?" Tempe watched the pacing woman.

"To get his stuff, sure."

"The marriage is over?"

"What do you think? You should have heard what he said before you came. Called me every name in the book. But I got him good. I told him I was going to take him for everything I could get. After what he did to me, any judge will see to it that I'm well taken care of."

For Jackie to threaten her husband wasn't very smart, but Tempe knew it wouldn't help to tell Jackie. "What did he say to that?"

Jackie lifted her pointed chin and smiled. "He wasn't happy, I can tell you. But all he said was, 'We'll see about that'."

Tempe finished her coffee and stood. "Look, if he comes back here and there's any trouble I want you to call 911."

"There's not going to be any trouble. Basically Tom's a coward. He's only brave enough to pick on someone like me. Now that everyone knows he's a wife beater, he wouldn't dare try anything else."

Jackie's eyes filled with tears and she began to sob. "I never thought it would end like this. I've loved Tom for a long, long time." She sighed. "I guess it's over for us."

"What's Ronnie up to?"

"Right now? It's not lunch time yet. He's still in bed." She wrinkled her nose.

"It might be a good idea to enlist your son's aid. When he does get up, ask him to stick around today, just in case."

She erupted with a loud cackle. "I'm afraid you don't know my Ronnie too well. He wouldn't lift a finger to help me. He hates me. Whenever Tom started hitting me, Ronnie couldn't get out of here fast enough. To be perfectly frank, I think he got a thrill out of knowing I was being hurt."

"If it's that bad, why do you let him live here?"

"What am I supposed to do? He hasn't got a job. I can't just throw out my own flesh-and-blood. I'm not heartless."

Tempe knew Jackie was a victim, and in this case, by her own choosing.

When Tempe left, she drove past a neighboring ranch-style home, one of the three houses in the cul-de-sac. She noticed a face in the front window before the lace curtain was hastily dropped back into place. Was that the curious neighbor, Yvette LaRue?

Hutch hadn't left for the hospital when she arrived home. "Great. You're here. You'll be able to go with me after all."

She shook her head. "I'm sorry, I can't. I have to be available for Jackie Cannata in case there's a problem." Tempe told Hutch about her meeting with Sergeant Guthrie, and what went on at the Cannatas'.

"But it sounds to me like everything is fine. Tom's gone out of town. Surely it won't matter if you go into Dennison for a couple of hours."

"Just because Tom said he was going out of town doesn't mean he really is. Once he starts thinking about Jackie's threats, he'll probably come back."

"Of course you know best. Did you suggest counseling to them?"

"Oh, yes. But at the moment, they're both very angry. Maybe they'll consider it later when they've calmed down some."

Hutch kissed her. "I'm sorry you can't go with me. I imagined your day off a bit differently. Thought we could go to lunch after our hospital visit, maybe take in a matinee."

"It's no longer a day off. At least the Sergeant is willing to pay me overtime."

"That means you'll be working later too?"

"Afraid so. I'll have to keep an eye on the Cannatas' place. I don't trust Tom to stay away, despite what he said."

Hutch pulled her close and hugged her. Though he didn't say so, she knew he was sorry that her job had made her lose faith in people.

When he released her, she recognized the sadness in his gray eyes, the same expression she always saw when he had doubts. Fortunately, there wasn't time for that discussion.

He smiled and kissed her again. "I love you, Tempe."

"And I love you."

They left the house at the same time, Tempe turning off the highway to make another swing around the Cannatas' cul-de-sac, and Hutch driving his old truck toward Dennison.

All was quiet on Aspen Road. Tempe decided to go into Bear Creek and for lunch at The Café. As she entered town, she recognized Tom's silver BMW backing out of a space in front of The Saloon. Pulling over, she watched Tom head up the highway toward the mountains. Obviously his business meeting hadn't been quite as urgent as he professed. She decided to go into The Saloon rather than follow him.

Housed in an old wooden building that dated from the early 1900's, the only bar in town was a popular gathering place. During the day, sandwiches and chips were served as well as drinks. Tempe recognized most of the faces that turned toward her as she entered. Near the middle of the long bar that ran the length of the narrow room were two men she knew worked on Cannata's construction crew.

"Hey, Deputy," Gus, the owner and bartender, hollered. He slid a plate with a thick sandwich and a bag of chips toward a husky man wearing a sleeveless black T-shirt that exposed bulging muscles. His long, dirty-blond hair was caught back by a rubber band. He picked up the sandwich and began eating, not looking at Tempe.

"Hi, guys. What's going on?" She headed toward the two men.

Chewing, the husky man continued to ignore her. On the other side of him, a redhead leaned back on his stool. "You want something from us?"

"I just saw your boss, Tom Cannata."

"Yeah." The husky one chomped on his sandwich.

"I wondered if he had anything interesting to say."

The redhead grinned. "Just the hundred or so ways he'd like to off his wife."

"Shut up," the husky one growled, nudging the redhead with his elbow.

"Hey! Mike, that hurt. What's the matter with you?" The redhead scowled. "You think...naw. It wasn't nothing like that. Tom's pissed. He was just mouthing off."

"Keep it to yourself, man." Making eye contact with Tempe for the first time since her approach, the muscular Mike said, "Tom's always talking bad about his old lady. It don't mean nothing."

"You want to tell me what he said?" Tempe asked.

"Naw. Don't even remember." Mike returned to devouring his sandwich.

"What about you, Gus? Did you hear what Tom Cannata said about his wife?"

Gus smoothed his walrus mustache. "Nah. I don't pay attention to that kind of trash." He turned away and began cleaning behind the bar.

Tempe stared at the construction workers. Mike's bulk completely hid the redhead from her view. She wasn't going to learn anything more from them. She waved an off-handed goodbye to Gus.

After her lunch at The Café, Tempe stopped by Cannatas' once again to chat with Jackie on the front porch. Yvette La Rue was weeding the flower garden in front of her house and glancing often in their direction.

"Would you look at Yvette? Who does she think she's fooling? She's got a yard man who does all that work for her." Jackie swept her blonde hair back from her face exposing the bruise that had turned an odd shade of green, the black stitches accenting her eyebrow. "Such a snoop. I'm surprised she doesn't trot her fat body on over here to ask what's going on."

Tempe wasn't interested in the feud between Jackie and her neighbor. "Remember, if Tom comes around, don't let him in. Give me a call and I'll get here right away."

"He won't be showing up here. He's away on business, remember?"

"Not yet, he isn't. I saw him in town a while ago." Tempe waited for her reaction.

Her hand flew to her injured face, "Oh. Well, there isn't anything to worry about...is there?"

"I don't know, Jackie. Is Ronnie up yet?"

"Up and gone."

"I told you to have him stick around."

Jackie shrugged. "I suggested that, but he had other things to do."

"Didn't you explain to him..."

Jackie interrupted, "Like I said, Ronnie and I don't get along."

"But you told me that he tried to get Tom to stop hitting you the other night."

Her voice rose. "So I lied. He didn't try to stop Tom. He watched for awhile...even had a smirk on his face. I think he'd celebrate if something bad happened to me."

"I doubt that," Tempe said, not believing her own words.

Jackie pointed toward her curious neighbor. "Look at that damn busybody. She's not even trying to hide the fact she's watching us."

Yvette stared openly toward Jackie's house, no longer going through the motions of weeding.

"Go in the house," Tempe instructed. "Lock the door. Don't open it unless you know who is out there. If Tom comes, call me. Don't let him in."

Jackie nodded though she took the time to glare for a long moment at Yvette, before disappearing into the house.

Tempe remained on the porch until she heard the deadbolt slide into place. She didn't put much faith in Jackie's promises either. Unfortunately, Jackie seemed far more concerned with her neighbor's inquisitiveness than her husband's threats.

There was nothing more Tempe could do for her. Though Jackie seemed unaware, Tempe's intuition, or Indian "hocus-pocus" as the Sergeant liked to call it, filled her with a sense of overpowering menace. Whether it was connected to Jackie or had something to do with Doretha's warning, Tempe didn't know.

Chapter 5

Tempe spent the afternoon as usual–cautioning speeders and issuing a few tickets, never straying far from Aspen Road. She ate a quick dinner with Hutch and Blair. Unable to relax, she hurried back to the Cannatas' to sit and drink coffee with a bored Jackie.

"How much longer do I have to hang around the house?" she asked.

"Until I'm sure Tom no longer poses a threat to you."

Jackie rolled her eyes. "That's not fair. I'm the victim here, but Tom's the one who can come and go as he pleases."

Having no answers for Jackie, Tempe again reminded her to keep the door locked, and left. She made her usual circuit above, through, and below Bear Creek until dark. Driving by the park, she spotted the glow from the tip of a cigarette and pulled up, thinking it might belong to Ronnie.

Still in fatigues, though he'd changed the olive green T-shirt for a black one, Ronnie didn't seem surprised when she approached him. "How goes it, Deputy? Catch any bad guys?"

"I've been checking on your Mom, Ronnie. You ought to be home with her."

Ronnie scowled fiercely. "I hate my mother."

"I realize kids think that sometimes, but you should put that aside for now. Tom is a real threat to her, you know."

Throwing down his cigarette and using the heel of his boot to grind it into the grass, Ronnie stood eye-to-eye with her. "Listen Deputy, I'm not going to play nursemaid to my mom. Tom can put her out of her misery for all I care."

"You don't mean that," Tempe said to Ronnie's back as he strode off toward the store. She climbed back in the Blazer to continue her rounds.

A three vehicle pile-up on the highway above Bear Creek kept

Tempe occupied for the next two hours. Finally able to leave, she glanced at her watch. Eleven forty-five. Time to make one last pass by Jackie Cannata's before going home to bed. She'd driven by regularly until the wreck. Jackie had told her she was going upstairs to watch television in bed. Ronnie would probably go home when he knew his mother was sleeping.

Though she had no basis for it, the oppressive menace Tempe felt earlier plagued her. She drove toward Aspen Road with a sense of urgency.

Rounding the corner into the cul-de-sac, she spotted black smoke swirling into the night sky. Jamming her foot down hard on the gas pedal, she sped toward Jackie's house. The smoke rolled out of a downstairs window.

"Oh, my God." Keying her mike, she reported the fire to the dispatcher, grabbed her flashlight, and jumped from the Blazer.

Darting across the lawn, she ran up the porch steps. At the door, she pounded on the polished oak, hollering, "Jackie! Open up! The house is on fire!" Surprisingly, the door opened easily when she turned the handle.

Though the smoke smell was strong, the flames seemed to be confined to the kitchen. Except for the sound of fire, the house was quiet. Neither Jackie nor Ronnie responded to her urgent cries of warning. She wondered if they'd already escaped. If so, where were they? And why hadn't they reported the emergency themselves?

"Jackie, Ronnie. Get out!" The only answer was the crackling flames. She pulled her shirt up over her nose and mouth, and crouching low, she headed up the stairs, taking shallow breaths in an attempt not to inhale much of the smoky air. Her legs seemed to be moving in slow motion. The higher she climbed, the denser and blacker the smoke.

At the top of the stairs, she crawled towards Jackie's bedroom. She hoped it was the right direction, but she could scarcely see.

Ever so often she called out, "Jackie...Ronnie," but nothing indicated either one heard her.

Reaching out, she touched a partially open door. It had to be the master bedroom. She flipped on her flashlight, following the strong beam bouncing off the dense smoke.

Where were the fire department and the volunteers?

"Jackie, if you're in there, come out now!"

The choking stench and roar of the flames were her only answer. She could think of no worse way to perish than to burn to death. She had to do whatever possible to rescue Jackie.

Flashlight under her arm, she crawled toward the bed.

A hand dangled off the side. Oh dear, God. "Jackie, can you hear me?"

Tempe's eyes stung as she knelt beside the bed. She pulled her onto the floor. "Wake up, Jackie. You've got to get out of here."

Jackie didn't respond. Tempe wasn't sure the woman was even breathing. She had to get her outside into the fresh air.

Dragging Jackie out of the room, toward the stairs, she wondered if Ronnie were in bed, but she could rescue only one at a time.

"Mom! Are you up there?"

Thank God. Blair! "I've got Jackie Cannata," she gasped, the smoke burning her throat. "Ronnie might be up here too."

Blair, in full turnout gear and breathing apparatus, appeared through the enveloping smoke. "Are you okay?"

"I think so. But Jackie isn't breathing."

Another firefighter emerged through the swirling blackness. "I'll take her." Tempe recognized the voice, Henley—cowboy and volunteer fireman.

"Where's Ronnie's bedroom? I'll go after him, and you need to get out of here now," Blair said.

Tempe pointed in the opposite direction from the master bedroom. "Please, be careful."

"Go, Mom." He disappeared into the swirling darkness.

Henley and another fireman headed down with Jackie. Tempe followed.

Before she reached the front door, Blair was beside her. "No one else is up there." She felt his arm around her as he pulled her out of the house. Tempe gulped in the fresh, sweet air and began coughing.

More firemen in their black, yellow-striped turnout gear and black helmets, aimed hoses at the flames erupting from the back part of the house. Windows shattered, and small explosions came from inside, startling Tempe. "What's that?" she asked between coughs.

"Aerosol cans. They always do that," Blair said. "How do you feel?"

Fire-storm wind blew through the burning structure, as they helplessly watched. The crackling and roar grew louder.

"I'm okay. Or at least I will be as soon as I get rid of all this smoke I've inhaled."

"You need to be checked out at the hospital."

That reminded her of Jackie. "Where's Mrs. Cannata?"

"There." Blair pointed to the edge of the lawn where Jackie lay on a gurney. Two firefighters stood beside her. Why weren't they doing anything?

Neighbors in nightclothes milled around outside the fence. Tempe noticed Yvette La Rue among them.

Hurrying to Henley's side, she asked, "What's going on? How is she?"

"Sorry, Deputy. She didn't make it. It wasn't the fire that got her."

"What?" Tempe moved closer. What could have happened?

Blonde hair fell over the bruised and stitched side of Jackie's face. Her eyes were open. She wore a white nightgown—the front was stained with a blossom of red around a dark hole in her chest.

"Looks like she was shot."

Oh, dear Lord. Tempe felt an instant pang of guilt and sadness for Jackie. "I'll have to call this in immediately." Preserving the crime scene was impossible—the fire was devouring it.

"Thought you might." Henley lifted his helmet and pushed back his hair. "I made a call to headquarters too. We need an arson investigator."

"I'm sure you're right." Tempe's mind reeled. Henley probably wasn't considering suicide...and she shouldn't either. She wondered where Tom Cannata was.

Henley returned to fight the fire.

Tempe turned to another volunteer firefighter and immediately recognized Charlene Goodsen, a wiry grandmother. "Can you give me a hand?"

"Sure, Tempe, what can I do?" The woman glanced toward the burning house. Tempe knew Charlene would much rather be firefighting.

"I'm going to have to call in a report...and I need to make sure that no one comes near the body. Will you stand guard, please?"

Though Charlene sighed, she said, "Of course, Deputy."

On the other side of the fence, the curious pressed closer to gawk at Jackie's body. When Tempe headed for the Blazer, Yvette La Rue separated herself from the others and waddled toward her.

"Deputy Crabtree, what's wrong with Jackie? Is she going to be all right?" Yvette's dimpled fingers clenched her purple chenille bathrobe over her ample bosom.

"I have something I have to do right now, but I'll talk to you in a moment." Tempe patted her pudgy arm.

"Oh."

Tempe made the call, knowing it would take nearly an hour for the homicide detectives to arrive at the scene. Both men lived in Visalia, and since it was the middle of the night, they'd have to dress first. She also requested that another deputy be dispatched to give her a hand.

❧❧

Hutch woke. He twisted and turned in the bed trying to find a comfortable spot. Reaching out for Tempe, he realized she wasn't there. The bed never felt quite right without her. What time was it, anyway? He glanced at the clock on the night stand. Nearly three! Something must have happened.

He tried to go back to sleep but knew that was impossible. The clock that never bothered him before ticked as loud as a metronome. It was so difficult not knowing what was going on and wondering if Tempe was in danger.

Getting up, he padded on bare feet to the window. All was quiet and peaceful. He ran his fingers through his hair, and sighed. Would he ever get used to her career?

If only it wasn't so important to her. Sometimes he had to fight the jealousy that came unbidden when the thought struck him that being a deputy came before anything else in Tempe's life. That wasn't true, he knew she loved him and Blair. But so often her job took priority over everything else.

The Cannata situation must have escalated. Perhaps Tom had attacked Jackie again. What was it Tempe told him? Domestic violence was the most dangerous call. Oh God, please don't let anything happen to Tempe.

Hutch dropped to his knees beside the bed, praying fervently until he returned to bed and fell into fitful slumber.

The sound of Tempe's squeaking leather belt woke him. He watched as she placed her handgun on the dresser. He squinted at the clock. It was after four. "Something must have happened. It's awfully late."

"Hi, honey. Sorry I woke you."

When she leaned over and kissed him, he smelled smoke. "Have you been at a fire?"

"Yeah. I'll tell you about it in the morning. I'm too tired to talk right now. I have to take a shower."

Hutch wanted to stay awake until she joined him in bed, but the sound of the running water lulled him back to sleep. No matter how hard he tried, he never seemed to be able to completely enter Tempe's world.

CHAPTER 6

Once again the incessant ringing of the phone woke Tempe. Why hadn't Hutch answered it? He must be gone. She glanced at the clock before she picked up the receiver—a few minutes past ten.

"Deputy Crabtree," she answered, stifling a yawn.

"Surprised I haven't heard from you already, Crabtree." It was Sergeant Guthrie. "Thought you'd be bugging me first thing about the arson report."

She became alert. "You got it already?"

"The prelim. Whoever shot the victim thought he could cover his tracks by burning the house. The fire was definitely started by an accelerant. We'll know more when the laboratory report comes in. The detectives didn't find any evidence of forced entry. They'll be back today to poke around some more. Make yourself available to them, Crabtree. I know they'll want to talk to you about the victim and her marital problems. Right now her husband is the most likely suspect."

Tempe sighed. "I worked until four this morning, Sergeant, on what was supposed to be my day off. Tuesdays I'm off too...do I get paid overtime? And when am I supposed to rest?"

"Yeah, yeah. I'll pick up the tab. You don't have to do any patrols—just head on over to the crime scene and give the detectives a hand. Shouldn't take too long. Okay?"

"Yes, sir."

"And by the way, Crabtree, where were you when all this was going on? You were supposed to be keeping an eye on the victim."

Tempe knew this was coming. She already felt guilty for not arriving at Cannatas' in time to prevent the murder. "I checked on her regularly, Sergeant, but I got involved with a big wreck. As soon as I was free, I went back to the Cannata residence. The house was on fire...and Jackie was dead."

The Sergeant didn't speak for a long while. When she was about to ask if he was still on the line, he said, "Yeah, well, I guess it couldn't be helped." But he didn't sound convinced. "Do whatever the detectives tell you but don't get in their way, okay?"

When she started brushing her black hair, the faint odor of smoke lingered. She decided against taking another shower because she might have to tramp around the ashes of what was left of the Cannatas' house.

She wondered where Ronnie had spent the night. That immediately brought the sickening thought that Ronnie might have killed his mother and set fire to the house.

She entertained the idea of putting on civilian clothes to get across to the detectives that she wasn't supposed to be working. But there was always the possibility they might want her to question someone, and it would be better to look official.

After donning her uniform, she braided her hair as usual, securing it to the back of her head with a silver barrette. Her fatigue began to dissipate as she fastened the utility belt around her waist. The excitement of being a part of the investigation took over.

The yellow crime scene tape drooped from where it had been strung across the front fence of the Cannata home. Thin wisps of smoke still spiraled upward from the blackened rubble. Parked beside a red fire truck was the nondescript Plymouth sedan that Tempe knew belonged to Morrison and Richards, homicide detectives from Tulare County Sheriff's Department.

Across the street staring in an openly curious manner were several Bear Creek residents, including Yvette LaRue.

Tempe spotted the tall, lean Richards standing at the front doorway that yawned into the ruined foyer. He wore a navy sport jacket, white shirt, and gray pants. He watched her approach. "Ah, good, Crabtree. Wanted to hear your view of this situation."

That was a new one. Usually neither of the detectives asked for her opinion about anything. Maybe, just maybe, the fact that she'd been right on a couple of their other cases had given them a different perspective, but probably that was too much to hope for.

"Well, I don't know who killed Jackie Cannata if that's what you're after, Lieutenant." She stepped up on the blackened, ash and debris strewn porch.

Richards squinted at her and passed a hand over his military-style haircut. He ignored her comment. "Heard you were the first one on the scene. What did you see when you got here?"

"The house was on fire. I reported it and went inside hoping to save Mrs. Cannata and her son."

"The door was open?"

"Not open but unlocked. That was strange because I'd been by several times earlier and I know Mrs. Cannata locked it carefully each time after I left."

Richards nodded. "Tell me about the son. I hear he wasn't in the house at the time of the fire. You got any idea where he might have been?"

"No, but I'm sure he'll turn up soon. Probably staying at a friend's house. He didn't get along with his mother."

"Yeah, we heard. Neighbors been talking to us already."

Morrison stepped through the doorway attempting to dust ashes off his brown corduroy jacket. "My money's on the kid. Getting to be a regular fad, kids killing their folks." His small eyes focused briefly on Tempe, but he didn't address her. Tempe knew his lack of greeting wasn't because he didn't like her. He was just rude. Built like a line-backer, his personality matched his ugly face.

Richards squinted at her again. "What do you think, Crabtree? Did the kid hate his mother enough to kill her? Did he have access to a weapon?"

"I don't know if he disliked her enough to kill her. I've known Ronnie since he was a youngster. He's always been different but that doesn't make him a murderer. I'm sure there were guns on the pre-mises and Ronnie would know where they were kept."

"Find the kid and we'll have our killer," Morrison growled.

"You do know about the husband ... that he spent the weekend in jail for battering his wife?" Tempe offered.

"Yeah, yeah." Morrison glared at the small crowd gathered across the street. "What's the matter with the people in this dinky town of yours? They got nothing better to do than hang around a crime scene? Maybe one of them had something to do with the fire. Fire bugs like to visit the scene of what they caused."

For the first time, Tempe took more than a perfunctory glance at the bystanders. Alongside Yvette were the folks who lived in the third house, the McKimsons, an elderly couple. Two young women from town held their toddlers by the hand. Standing off to the side, half-hidden by the branches of a weeping willow, Tempe recognized Spence Gullott. He adjusted his thick glasses and moved backwards even more into the protective shelter of the tree that drooped over the road at the side of LaRue's yard. Tempe wondered if anyone had questioned him about his whereabouts last night.

Smiling at Morrison, Tempe said, "We don't have a lot of excitement up here in Bear Creek. It's not like down there in the valley where you have shootings almost every night."

Both men ignored her comment. Richards said, "The husband has an alibi. He's been located at the Radisson in Fresno. There for some kind of meeting. He's on his way back as we speak."

"He told me yesterday morning he was leaving town." Tempe reached back to check her barrette.

"See...he's got an alibi," Morrison said.

"Except he also told me he was leaving right then and I saw him a little later heading into the mountains," Tempe said.

"So, he went wherever he was going first then out of town."

"He was really angry with his wife. It wouldn't hurt to call the hotel and see if he was actually registered last night," Tempe suggested.

Morrison's face turned uglier as he glared at her. "We know how to do our job, Crabtree." He moved closer to her. Despite her 5' 8", this extremely big man always made Tempe feel small, but mainly it was because of his patronizing attitude.

"Reason why we wanted you here was because we've got a job for you," Richards said. "You always manage to horn in on our murder investigations anyway, so thought we'd keep you out of our hair by giving you something to do," Richards said.

Tempe fought hard to keep from showing her anger. She'd solved more than one murder case for them though they'd never admit it. She pulled a notebook from her pocket. "How can I be of help?"

"Start by talking to the neighbors. See if anyone saw anything suspicious last night. Keep your eye out for the kid. Let us know the minute you spot him. We'll take care of him after that."

"Before I begin," Tempe said, "there's something else you should know. See that man standing over there by the willow tree?"

Morrison shaded his eyes. "I don't see anyone."

"I do," Richards said. "There's some guy way back in the shadows. What about him?"

"His name is Spence Gullott. He and Tom Cannata have a disagreement over a pond."

"But it was Mrs. Cannata who got killed," Morrison pointed out.

"It could have been a way to get back at Tom," Tempe suggested. She didn't think that was the case, but the detectives ought to be considering all the possibilities no matter how remote.

Morrison rolled his tiny eyes. "Don't worry about trying to solve the crime, Crabtree. Just get the information and pass it on. That's all I'm asking. Think you can handle it?"

"Yes, sir."

"And, Crabtree," Morrison began. "Lay off Tom Cannata. He's got influential friends."

Tempe couldn't keep herself from stating, "I wonder if his 'influential friends' know he battered his wife on a regular basis?" as she headed toward the gathered neighbors.

Yvette waddled over to meet her in the middle of the street. Her plump body was covered by an oversize, lime green sweat suit. "Do they know who did it yet? Oh, it's just so awful! Poor Jackie. We've known each other for years. I can't believe she's gone."

When the woman paused for a breath, Tempe said, "I need to ask you some questions"

A dimpled hand flew to Yvette's breast. "My goodness, I don't have a clue about what happened."

"Did you notice anything unusual?"

She vigorously shook her head. "I was sound asleep until I heard the sirens."

Tempe noticed Spence Gullott loping toward a bright red Suburban, no license, a new purchase sticker in the window. Waving at him, she hollered, "Hey, Gullott! Hold on a second." She turned back to Yvette. "Stick around. I still want to talk to you."

Spence stopped beside the open driver's door of the Suburban, appearing ready to bolt at any moment.

"Hey! Nice car," she said, as she caught up to him. "When did you get this?"

"Last week." A tic beneath his eye jumped into action.

"You must be doing okay."

"Is that what you wanted to talk to me about? How my business is doing? Though I don't see how it can be any of your concern, if you must know, I have more work than I need."

"I wondered what you were doing up here." Tempe moved closer so she could view the interior of the Suburban. She remembered Spence's other vehicle, an old Volvo station wagon. It had been full of clutter—computers, printers and boxes chock full of papers and books. Obviously he hadn't had this one long enough to load it with the tools of his profession.

"Curious, that's all. I came to find out what happened up here. Heard the sirens last night, smelled the smoke. I live right below Cannatas' property, as you well know."

"Below Tom's pond."

She'd struck a nerve. The tic quickened its pace. "Yeah, well, that pond's gotta go, even if I have to blow it up."

"That wouldn't be wise, would it? If you blew it up, the water would dump right on your house. Isn't that your big concern?"

Spence's long, dour face turned ashen. "That was merely a figure of speech. Of course I don't have any such notion."

"Now that the Cannatas' house burned down and Jackie is dead, I wonder if Tom is still interested in this piece of property and the pond." Tempe watched Spence carefully.

His already protruding eyes bugged even further behind the thick lenses of his glasses. As though he might be having difficulty breathing, Spence gasped out, "Oh, my God! You don't think...no...never. I can't believe...surely not..."

"What are you talking about Mr. Gullott?"

Spence gulped air and regained some of his composure. "Listen here, Deputy Crabtree, I'm not stupid and it wouldn't take an Einstein to figure out what you're intimating. Granted I'm not crazy about Tom, and I hate his stupid pond, but I had nothing against his wife. No matter what, I would never ever take someone's life. Why...I don't even own a gun!"

"How did you know Jackie was shot?"

The blood drained from his face. "I don't ... I don't know," he sputtered. "Maybe I heard someone talking about it...that busybody LaRue woman...she was blabbing about the murder to everyone."

Though that was certainly possible, Tempe didn't intend to cross him off her list of suspects yet. He didn't seem the type to pay attention to gossip or even spend time talking to Yvette. It wasn't necessary for the murderer to own a gun. She had a hunch the murder weapon had been readily available in the victim's bedroom.

CHAPTER 7

Yvette LaRue seemed thrilled to be questioned by Tempe, she fluttered her eyelashes, glancing at the young mothers with their children and the elderly couple as if to make sure they noticed she'd been singled out.

"I'd love to help in anyway that I possibly can, Deputy. I'd so hoped to renew my friendship with Jackie." She sniffled and wiped her eyes with a tissue she pulled from the pocket of her sweat pants. "Now it will never happen."

Afraid Yvette might dissolve in tears, Tempe quickly asked, "Did you notice anything unusual around here last evening? Any cars that you didn't recognize?"

"I have to confess I did sort of keep my eye on Jackie's place. Saw your Blazer parked in the driveway several times. No suspicious cars though. Of course there could have been one. I went into the kitchen and fixed snacks for me and Emory and sometimes I got interested in what was on the TV."

"What about Mr. Cannata. Did you see his BMW around here last night?"

"Now that you mention it, you know, I think I did." She grabbed Tempe's arm. "Oh, my goodness...you don't think? Surely not. But after the way he treated her anything's possible, isn't it?"

"Do you know when you saw Tom's car?"

Yvette screwed her chubby face into a frown, her eyes staring upward as she considered her answer. "I believe it was just before I went to bed. Yes, it was the last time I peeked out the window."

"And, do you have any idea of the time?" Tempe prompted.

She grinned proudly. "Oh, sure. It was 11:30. Emory and I had just finished watching the news. We always watch the eleven o'clock news and then go to bed."

"Did you actually see Tom get out of his car and go into the house?"

The smile disappeared. "Well, no. The car was there when I looked out. It hadn't been when I looked before, but that time it was." She shrugged her shoulders. "Sorry."

"That's all right. What about Ronnie? Jackie's son."

"Oh, that kid. What a mess. If I had a boy like that I certainly wouldn't allow him to dress like one of those fanatic military weirdoes. The way he sneaks in and out of that house at all hours, there's no telling what he's up to. I'm sure he doesn't have a job or go to school. I wouldn't trust that kid any farther than I could throw him."

"What I meant was...did you see Ronnie last night?"

"No, can't say as I did. He wasn't in the house last night was he? Maybe he was the one who did it. I wouldn't put anything past that kid. Always scowling and sneaking about like a spy or a crook."

"I really want to talk to Ronnie. If he comes around, give me a call, will you?" Tempe wrote her home phone number on a card and handed it to Yvette. She beamed at Tempe.

"Thank you, Mrs. LaRue. You've been very helpful." Tempe left noting that Yvette stepped closer to the young mothers.

The McKimsons were no longer on the sidewalk and Tempe guessed they had returned to their home, a modest, stucco, forties-style bungalow. At Tempe's knock, Mr. McKimson opened the door. He was slim and straight, and neatly attired in a crisply ironed, patterned long-sleeved shirt and khaki work pants. Tempe guessed he was in his late seventies.

He appeared startled by her unexpected appearance. His white brows shot up over wide eyes. "Oh," he said. When he gathered his composure, he added, "Deputy. Goodness, we didn't expect you. Please, come in."

Mrs. McKimson hovered close behind him. A head shorter, her white hair in a simple ear-length page-boy, she too was slim though slightly hunched. "Can I get you a cup of coffee or tea?"

Tempe stepped into the neat living room. The furniture consisted of a matching Danish-style couch and love seat upholstered in a leafy print fabric, chairs and tables, all probably fifty years old. Framed pictures of children and grandchildren set on every available surface.

"No. No, thanks. I just have a couple of questions to ask."

After listening to their expressions of sorrow and horror about

Jackie Cannata's fate, it only took a moment for her to realize the McKimsons knew nothing helpful. Their regular bedtime was eight-thirty. They had been awakened by the sirens. They were unaware of anything that had gone on at their neighbors' between the time they retired and were aroused by the noise.

Tempe quickly relayed what she'd discovered to the detectives. Before they dismissed her, Morrison mumbled, "I don't care what anyone says, I still think it was the kid that did in his mother. You find him for us, Crabtree, and I bet he'll confess."

Since he didn't give her specific orders, Tempe went home. She was disappointed that Hutch's old blue truck was missing from the driveway. It always helped to run her ideas by him. Unlike Morrison, she hoped Ronnie had nothing to do with his mother's death. She would like to talk to him before the detectives located him.

She parked the Blazer. As she unlocked the back door of their rustic cottage, she wondered if they would ever find the time to re-model the place as they so often dreamed. She couldn't imagine living anywhere else. The house perched above the river. No matter what else was going on, the sound of the water rushing over the rocky bed never failed to soothe her.

Stepping inside, she glanced around the old-fashioned kitchen, expecting to find a note, but there wasn't one. If Hutch were going to Dennison, he usually left a message. He must be around Bear Creek somewhere. Just in case, Tempe checked the calendar hanging on the rough hewn wooden cabinet. Nothing was written on the date. However, she saw that he had an out-of-town meeting scheduled for the weekend. She remembered Hutch telling her about it, a conference for ministers of small, rural churches. He was excited about attending.

The light on the answering machine blinked. Tempe dreaded pushing the key to listen to it. She didn't need another emergency to keep her from using the remainder of her day off in her own way.

But she pressed the key and listened absently, expecting to hear the Sergeant's voice, or perhaps one of Bear Creek's residents who didn't like dealing with a substitute deputy. Instead, a strange voice spoke, gravelly and harsh, almost as though the person were disguising it.

"You better mind your own business, Deputy Crabtree, or you'll be sorry."

Frowning, Tempe rewound the tape and played it again. What a stupid message. Minding other people's business was part of her job. And what did the "or you'll be sorry" mean? Obviously it was a threat, but how real? She rewound it again and listened a third time, hoping to recognize the voice but nothing was familiar about it.

She plucked the tape from the machine and dropped it into the pocket of her shirt, replacing it with a new one. Next time she went to Dennison she would take the tape with its enigmatic message to Sergeant Guthrie. She thought it nothing to worry about—probably just some kids with nothing better to do.

Hurrying down the narrow hall, past Blair's room, she went into the bedroom to change clothes. She wanted to do a few household chores. It wasn't long before she had forgotten the tape and the cryptic message.

✿❦

Hutch called in mid-afternoon. He'd been working at the chapel. "Glad to know you're home. You do have the rest of the day off, don't you?"

"So far," Tempe said.

"Why don't we go out for dinner?" he suggested. "Remember, I'll be out of town all weekend."

"That sounds like a good idea. At least we won't be interrupted if we eat away from home. I'll find something in the freezer for Blair. Where did you want to go?"

"Unless you want hamburgers, where else is there but the Inn?"

"Do you want me to make a reservation?"

"Yes, please. I have quite a bit to do here in the office before I'm free, but ought to be home about five."

When Blair came in from school, he seemed happy that Hutch and Tempe wouldn't be home that evening. "Hey, great. I don't have any homework. Think I'll head up to the fire station after I grab a bite."

"What about finals? Shouldn't you be studying?"

He grinned at her. "Don't worry, Mom. I've got it under control."

She realized he probably did. It was hard for her to accept her son had grown so much in the last couple of years.

✿❦

The log building that housed the inn began as a stage coach stop. It had been remodeled and turned into a hotel in the '30s. In the '70s it was further expanded into a restaurant and lodge. Claudia Donato, the latest owner of Bear Creek Inn, led Tempe and Hutch across the worn, hardwood floor that gleamed with polish, into the large dining room to their favorite table near the original massive stone fireplace. Rough cut logs used as beams crisscrossed the cathedral high ceiling.

Hutch seated Tempe at the white linen covered table. A centered crystal vase held freshly cut yellow rosebuds from the Inn's garden. Claudia smiled and handed each of them an oversized menus. As usual, the woman's shoulder-length blonde hair was artfully tousled, her make-up perfect. She recited a list of specials and left them to make their decision.

A young waitress appeared and took their order. Once she'd left them alone, Hutch began talking about his up-coming trip, his enthusiasm evident.

"I hope you have a wonderful time," Tempe said.

He reached across the table and squeezed her hand, "I just wish you could go with me. It will be the first time we've been apart."

"It would take an act of God for me to get a weekend off, especially a holiday weekend." She laughed. "It's hard enough to keep the two days I'm supposed to have."

"True enough."

The food arrived, and they concentrated on their meal for a few moments. "How's yours?" Hutch asked.

"Wonderful, as usual." She glanced out the window in time to see Ronnie Keplinger dashing across the highway.

Tossing her napkin aside, she said, "Excuse me, Hutch, there's something I have to do."

"Goodness, Tempe, finish your dinner first." Hutch frowned.

"Sorry. This is important."

Heedless of the startled glances of the other diners, Tempe jogged toward the entrance of the Inn, thankful she'd worn flat pumps and an outfit with pants instead of a skirt.

Claudia gaped, open-mouthed. "Is something wrong?"

"No, nothing," Tempe said, pushing against the heavy, ornately carved door.

She bounded down the steps and to the road. Ronnie was no longer in sight, but he couldn't have gone far.

Watching out for traffic, she darted across the highway and into the park. Ronnie was nowhere to be seen. Damn! She'd interrupted her dinner for nothing. Hutch would be upset.

When she returned to the table, she smiled apologetically.

"What on earth was that all about?" he asked.

Still breathing heavily from her exertion, she said, "I saw Ronnie Keplinger, and I need to talk to him." She picked up her fork.

"Is what you have to say to him so important that it has to interfere with what precious little time we have together?"

She put the fork down on her plate. "I really am sorry, but I don't know where he's staying."

Hutch's demeanor didn't soften. "If you don't find him before, you can always talk to him at the funeral. It's going to be Thursday morning at the chapel."

It was Tempe's turn to be irritated. "Tom called you? Why didn't you tell me?"

"I hadn't got around to it."

"Tell me now," Tempe said, no longer hungry. She pushed her plate aside.

The freckles on Hutch's cheeks darkened. "Tom called me at the chapel this morning, wanting to make arrangements for the service and his wife's burial."

"Did he say where he was calling from?"

Hutch shook his head. "No, Tempe, that didn't come up in our conversation."

"How did he sound?"

"Not upset, if that's what you mean. Actually, he was quite business-like and knew exactly what he wanted."

Tempe nodded.

"But that doesn't mean anything," he added quickly. "Some folks conceal their true feelings when they are making funeral arrangements. Sometimes taking care of all the details is what keeps them together."

"I doubt that Tom is broken up about Jackie, angry as he was with her yesterday," Tempe said.

"Sounds as though you've made up your mind that he killed Jackie."

"No, I haven't. But I do think he's a better candidate than Ronnie."

Hutch frowned. "Surely no one is suggesting that Ronnie murdered his own mother."

"That's what Detective Morrison thinks."

"Why?"

"In his case, I suspect it's a gut instinct more than anything. The unfortunate part is that if he knew as much about Ronnie as I do, he'd be even more convinced."

"I guess I understand why you want to talk to him. But it's so maddening that we can't have a pleasant meal together without you job intruding."

"I know."

The waitress approached the table. "Can I interest you in some dessert?"

Hutch raised an auburn eyebrow at Tempe. "No, we've finished here."

He paid the check.

Though the romantic mood had been shattered, and she was to blame, Tempe hoped it could be restored. "Why don't we go home?"

On the way out to the truck, she took Hutch's hand.

He said, "I wish your job didn't interfere so much with our life."

For the moment, she felt the same way. "Me too." And it was far more complicated than her mind being on Jackie Cannata's murder. Her thoughts were never far from the job. It was impossible to disengage the deputy part of her life when she wasn't on duty. A piece of her was always on alert. She felt guilty.

He held the door open for her, then came around to the driver's side. "You seem so preoccupied. Is it the murder, or something else?"

CHAPTER 8

"You do know me pretty well, don't you?"

"So what is it, something I can help with?" Hutch checked the traffic, and pulled out onto the highway.

"I'll probably have to work it out myself," Tempe said.

"Why not tell me about it? After all, listening to people's problems is a major part of my job."

"I only wish I'd stayed with Jackie last night. That's what I was supposed to be doing, protecting her. If I'd been there, she'd still be alive."

"Didn't a bad accident keep you away?"

"Yes, but I shouldn't have responded. I should have just left it to someone else."

"I can't imagine your ignoring an accident under any circumstances. You couldn't have predicted that someone would kill Jackie Cannata and set her house on fire while you were gone."

"I realize all that. I've given myself the same argument over and over, but it doesn't change the fact that if I'd been there things would have been different. I can't help it, Hutch, I feel responsible."

"Oh, sweetheart, no wonder you've been so preoccupied." He made the turn onto the road that crossed the river and in moments parked the truck next to the Blazer.

He hurried around to the front and took her into his arms as she slid out. "Sweetheart, you didn't have any control over the one who pulled the trigger. If the murderer didn't kill Jackie last night because you were there, he would have kept on trying until he succeeded. You know that."

And she did. Though she'd considered those same phrases herself, Hutch gave them affirmation. Along with his reassurance, she felt the warmth of his love.

"Thank you," she whispered in his ear.

As soon as they stepped inside the house and Hutch pushed the door closed, he circled her with his arms and bent to kiss her. The moment was interrupted by the sound of Blair's VW bug coming to a stop in front.

Tempe grinned at Hutch. "Never fails."

"If we hurry, we could be in the bedroom before he comes in." Hutch grinned mischievously.

Torn by her desire to be with her husband and the need to question her son, Tempe said, "You go on. I have to talk to Blair."

Hutch kissed her again. "Couldn't it wait until morning?"

"Probably. But I promise, I'll be right there."

Hutch shrugged and caressed her cheek with the back of his hand before disappearing down the hall.

Blair seemed surprised to see Tempe standing in the kitchen. "You weren't waiting for me, were you? It's still really early."

"No, sweetheart. I wanted to ask you something."

"Okay." Blair opened the refrigerator, gazing inside.

"Do you have any idea where Ronnie Keplinger might be staying?"

"Not really, but I just saw him."

"Where?"

"Going into the market." Blair brought out a carton of milk and a dish holding the last of an apple pie. "That's why I came home. Got hungry and I didn't have any money."

"Listen, Blair, would you mind telling Hutch that I've gone out for a minute?"

Blair tipped his head and frowned. "I've got an idea this isn't going to make him too happy. Why don't you tell him yourself?"

Her hand on the doorknob, Tempe said, "If you explain I've gone to see Ronnie Keplinger, he'll understand." She was out the door before her son could argue further.

Of course she didn't know whether Hutch would understand even though they had been discussing Ronnie earlier in the evening. But she couldn't relax knowing she'd passed up the opportunity to question Ronnie. Whether or not she'd take him in for questioning, depended upon what he told her.

She arrived at the market just as Ronnie stepped out, a bag of groceries in his hand. He looked startled when she drove the Blazer alongside him, and for a moment she thought he might bolt. Leaning across the seat, she opened the passenger door. "Get in, Ronnie."

He eyed her suspiciously. "What for?"

"I want to talk to you for a minute. It won't take long."

With obvious reluctance, he climbed in and pulled the door closed. Tempe drove only a few yards, parking near the fire station.

"I'm sorry about your mother, Ronnie."

"Yeah...me too." He shook his head. "I hated the way she acted...never standing up to Tom. But I didn't want anything like this to happen to her."

A tear eased down the side of Ronnie's nose, and he quickly wiped it away. He stared out the window.

"I'd like to ask some questions about last night, Ronnie."

Keeping his head turned, he said, "Sure."

"Where were you, anyway?"

"Mom and I got into a fight...as usual...and I stormed out of there."

"Where did you go?"

"Nowhere particular."

"Ronnie, did your mother have a gun?"

"She didn't, but Tom had lots of them."

"Where did he keep them?"

"Everywhere. Mom had one of them on the stand beside the bed last night. Maybe she was expecting trouble."

"I know she was afraid of Tom," Tempe offered. "What kind of gun was it, Ronnie?"

Ronnie hunched his shoulders. "A revolver...small caliber."

"Was it loaded?"

"I'm sure it was. What would be the point of having it, if it wasn't?"

The gun ought to be somewhere in the ruins of the house. Tempe wondered if the arson people or the detectives found it—and if it was the murder weapon.

Tempe had one more question to ask. "When you left, Ronnie, did you lock the door?"

He scowled at her. "No, I didn't lock the door. I told you I was mad. All I wanted to do was get out of there." His expression underwent an obvious change.

"Aw, shit! That's how the murderer got in, isn't it?"

He seemed so stricken, Tempe offered an answer to ease his pain. "If your step-father did it, he had a key, so it wouldn't have mattered."

"I ought to kill the bastard."

Tempe put a restraining hand on his arm. "That wouldn't help, Ronnie. We don't know that it was Tom."

"Who else hated her enough?"

At times, Ronnie had sounded as though he did, but if Morrison could operate on instinct, so could she, and she didn't think Ronnie killed his mother no matter how he spouted off about her.

"We'll leave it up to the detectives to find that out. Have you heard about the funeral yet? It's Thursday morning at Bear Creek chapel."

"Thanks for telling me. Is that all?"

Tempe knew she ought to take Ronnie in so the detectives could question him. But if she did, he'd have to spend a night in jail. Knowing how Morrison felt about him, it might be even longer. "Listen, Ronnie, the detectives on the case want to talk to you. Where are you staying so I can tell them?"

"I'll give you a call in the morning, Deputy. I'm kind of moving from place to place."

Tempe didn't know if she could trust him. "Don't leave Bear Creek."

"I'm not planning on it. I'll be around." He was out of the car and loped down the highway before she could stop him.

When she returned home, Blair had gone to bed. Entering her bedroom, she found Hutch sitting up in bed, his Bible open on his lap. He peered at her over the top of his glasses. "Well...you finally got back. Did you learn anything worthwhile?"

Though he didn't sound annoyed, she wondered if he were angry that she'd taken off without an explanation. She would be under similar circumstances. "Yes, actually I did. I'm convinced Ronnie had nothing to do with his mother's death."

"Good, I'm glad to hear it." He stared at the Bible, but she didn't think he was reading it because he didn't turn the page.

She undressed quickly and put on her nightgown.

"Of course, that means you, or someone, must still find out who is guilty."

"Hopefully, it will be the detectives. They certainly have told me enough times to stay out of their way." Tempe slipped into bed beside him.

"Except when they want you to do something." He continued to stare at the Bible propped against his knees.

"True." Tempe cuddled against him, but he remained rigid. She nibbled on his ear.

Hutch shut the Bible and put it on the table. He took off his glasses and put them on the Bible. "I do wish your job didn't interfere so much with our life." He slid his arms around her.

She was glad it was hard for him to stay mad.

⚘

The next morning as Hutch prepared to leave for the hospital to look in on Clare, he said, "I have a meeting later to finalize plans with Tom about Jackie's funeral."

The information gave Tempe an idea. "When and where is it? I'd like to ask him a few questions and I have no idea where he's staying."

Hutch frowned. "Is that appropriate?"

She shrugged. "Appropriate or not, it's likely Tom killed his wife. The detectives will expect me to know how to locate him."

No sooner had Hutch left when the phone rang. It was Sergeant Guthrie. "Thought I'd let you in on the latest. Cannata's alibi doesn't check out."

"He wasn't at the business meeting?"

"Oh, he turned up at the meeting all right—that's where we found him to give him the news about his wife. What he didn't do was check into the hotel. He had a reservation, but he never showed up to get the key."

"So that makes him the number one suspect, right?"

"I'd say so. That's Richard's call, but Morrison still thinks it's the kid."

"I'm just as positive he's not."

"Does that mean you've seen the kid?"

"Actually I did run into Ronnie last night."

"Didn't Morrison tell me you were supposed to bring Ronnie in for questioning if you spotted him?"

"Oh, was I?"

"You know doggone good and well that's what you were supposed to do. No harm done. You can pick him up this morning."

"Well, Sergeant, actually I can't."

"Why not?" Guthrie sounded irritated.

"Because I don't know where he's staying."

The sergeant sputtered and mumbled a string of expletives.

"Don't worry, he'll be at the funeral tomorrow."

"You better be right."

Immediately after the Sergeant hung up, the phone rang again.

"Deputy Crabtree," she answered.

Tempe recognized Doretha Nightwalker's low voice immediately even though the shaman didn't identify herself. "I'm continuing to receive dark feelings about you. Can you come over this morning?"

CHAPTER 9

"You want me to come to your house?" Tempe glanced at her watch. She had plenty of time.

"If that's possible. I think it's vital," Doretha said.

Curiosity more than anything prompted Tempe to agree. "I'll leave now."

It didn't take long for Tempe to reach the road across from the entrance to the campground by the lake, a narrow road that meandered up and down, over the hills leading toward Bear Creek Indian Reservation. On her way she passed orchards of oranges, plums, and kiwi, separated by cattle ranches, large and small. Mobile homes were scattered between two-story clapboard houses, contemporary low-slung stuccos, and an occasional newly-constructed log cabin. Several times, the road crossed over a branch of Bear Creek.

The hills, a patchwork of yellow, gold, orange and greens, seemed to grow in size as she neared her destination. The ranches were bigger, the houses farther apart. Several times she rattled across cattle guards, and once she stopped for a cowboy on horseback driving a small herd of cattle across the road.

All the while she thought about the shaman, wondering what was so urgent.

A rock wall marked the way into the reservation. A hand carved sign proclaimed that Ulysses S. Grant instituted the reservation in 1873. It was nestled among oaks, poplars and cottonwoods in a verdant valley backed by the snow-covered peaks of the Sierra.

Bear Creek Mission, the Indian Education Center, a modern fire station, and several one-story buildings on both sides of the road sported signs that told of the services offered inside. Small houses, no two-alike, dotted the hillsides.

Tempe followed one of the many roads crisscrossing the reservation, arriving at Doretha's small two-story home tucked away in a wooded setting. Weeping willows dangled fronds over gray, granite boulders. Tall grasses and flowers grew in a random pattern beside the stone walkway.

Before Tempe could knock, the door opened.

Doretha radiated strength and dignity. A long-sleeved multi-colored embroidered tunic fell loosely past her slim hips, and a dark green, broomstick skirt reached nearly to her sandaled feet. Dark, determined eyes narrowed briefly as the woman seemed to examine Tempe before greeting her. "Ah, it's good to see you. Come in."

Tempe stepped into the plant filled entry. Doretha ushered her past a simple staircase that led to the upper floor and into the living room filled with a mixture of antiques. Tempe settled herself among the brightly colored pillows on the blue-and-white patterned couch as Doretha sat on the ancient, carved wood-and-leather rocker near the French doors flung open to the outside. Shimmery white curtains fluttered in the breeze.

"What's this all about, Doretha?" Tempe asked.

Instead of answering the question, the shaman asked one of her own. "Tell me, Tempe, have things changed for you in any way since you've been more in touch with your beginnings?"

"Actually, they have. I can't really explain, but I seem to be more aware of everything."

A smile played on Doretha's lips, as she rocked rhythmically. "If you would spend more time learning and experiencing the old ways you'd find yourself perceiving all things in the truest manner."

Tempe lifted her eyebrows slightly. "You know how my husband feels about that."

"Don't use him as an excuse. I told you I had the distinct feeling that he's coming around."

Tempe remained skeptical, but that didn't matter.

"I believe he's beginning to understand his beliefs and mine are far more compatible than he originally thought. He agrees we are serving the same Creator. Don't discount him, my dear."

Tempe didn't know how to respond because she certainly did not discount her husband about anything. She did know what upset him, however. Some things, like her job, she had no control over, but Native American spiritual beliefs were a different matter.

Doretha quickly continued. "Over the years, I've learned to pay attention to my feelings and, as I told you, a great foreboding about you has been disturbing my dreams as well as my waking hours."

"What does that mean?" Tempe asked. She'd certainly experienced similar sensations herself many times.

"Unfortunately, I can't perceive any details. I know that you are in grave danger, and that danger is growing stronger all the time. I can't help but wonder if you are living the life the Creator intended for you."

"That I am sure about. Being a deputy isn't just what I do. Doretha, it's what I am."

Doretha rocked back and forth, studying Tempe all the while. "Since you obviously have no doubts, then we must solve your problem in another way."

"What would you suggest?" Tempe asked.

"We should call the sacred powers to be with you."

"And how do we do that?"

"We'll have a special ceremony. Similar to a vision quest."

Tempe glanced at her watch. "Right now?"

"Night time is better, when we can draw on the strength of the stars. Could you come back this evening?"

Tempe shook her head. "No, I have to work. Besides, no matter how you may think Hutch has changed, I know he isn't ready for me to participate in another ceremonial, whatever the reason."

Doretha rose from the rocking chair, crossed the gleaming plank floor and reached for Tempe's hands. "This is critical to your well-being. No, that's not strong enough. You must do it for your life."

Tempe didn't doubt that Doretha believed what she was saying. Though Tempe had given credence to the power of Native American mysticisms because of her own experience, she wasn't ready to accept the notion that participating in an ancient ritual could protect her from anything. She put her faith in her own skills, and her service revolver.

"It isn't possible any time soon."

Continuing to grip Tempe's hands, Doretha said, "You must make time."

Tempe shook her head. "I don't know." She remembered Hutch would be out of town this weekend ... but it was the Memorial Day holiday. Things were likely to get crazy. Because of the holiday, as well as more highway patrol, an extra deputy would be assigned to the area. "Maybe after I get off work Friday. It will be awfully late."

"I hope it's not too late. Until then you must be extremely careful." Doretha stepped back.

Tempe stood. "I'll try to make it, really I will."

"I won't accept that. You must promise me that you will come here Friday night. No matter how late it is, I'll be waiting."

❧❧

Driving back on the winding road away from the reservation, Tempe sighed as she thought about the commitment she'd made to Doretha. After dealing with all the problems that were sure to crop up with the locals and the many visitors determined to have a good time, Tempe knew she wouldn't be interested in making the long drive back to the reservation at the end of her shift. On the other hand, if participation in the ceremonial could guarantee her safety—. Tempe shook her head. It was too far out even to consider. But then again, in spite of her doubts, she had been able to call back a spirit from the dead.

Not only had the spirit explained her own death, she'd saved Tempe's life.

The only thing to do was wait and see what occurred Friday night. At least Hutch would be gone and she wouldn't have to listen to his objections to the plan.

She made a right turn onto the highway and headed toward Bear Creek, instinctively keeping an eye on the traffic around her. Ahead she spotted a familiar car—a silver BMW, Tom Cannata's. It was moving fast enough to warrant a traffic stop.

Turning on the Blazer's light bar brought the other vehicle to the side of the road.

Tom lowered the window when she reached the driver's door. He screwed up his face. "Not you again. What is it this time?"

"First, I'd like to offer my sympathies on the death of your wife."

His dark eyebrows leaped upward. "That's what you stopped me for? Couldn't you wait until the funeral?"

"I stopped you because you were going ten miles over the speed limit."

"You know as well as I do, that everyone does."

"That doesn't make it right."

Tom shook his head.

"Where were you the night your wife was killed?"

"I don't think that's really any of your concern. I've spent plenty of time talking to those detectives. But if you must know, I was out of town on business."

"Where is out of town?"

"The Ramada Inn in Fresno."

"I heard you had a reservation but didn't show up until the next day."

A brief shadow darkened Tom's eyes but he quickly regained his self-control. "Think what you like, Deputy."

"Your neighbor, Mrs. LaRue, told me she saw your BMW parked outside your house around eleven the night of the fire."

Tom's complexion changed from tan to an unhealthy purple. "That woman is a liar!"

"What reason would she have to lie?"

"How the hell would I know? If you're going to give me a ticket, get on with it."

She did just that.

≈≈

When Tempe stepped inside the kitchen, she immediately noticed the red light flashing on her answering machine and listened to the message while taking off her utility belt.

Again, a disguised husky voice breathed, "Keep your nose out of other people's business or you'll be sorry!"

Tempe played it again and listened carefully. She still couldn't recognize the voice but felt sure it was being disguised somehow. One thing she did know was that the threat was meant to make her back-off from investigating Jackie's murder.

She smiled. If she wouldn't cease her unauthorized snooping on orders from Sergeant Guthrie, why would she take the suggestion of an unknown coward who left cryptic threats on an answering machine? Whoever it was would certainly have to come up with something more menacing.

CHAPTER 10

Most of the residents of Bear Creek came to Jackie Cannata's funeral. Not surprisingly, Sergeant Guthrie gave Tempe the job of watching for anything unusual. Because of her official role, she wore her uniform. Of course the assignment was unnecessary. She would have attended and observed everyone's behavior without orders to do so.

Wreaths, bouquets and potted plants surrounded the white coffin in front of the altar. Though nearly every pew in the sanctuary was crowded, sadly, the front row reserved for the family of the deceased was empty. Where were Tom and Ronnie?

A friend of Jackie's sang the first song. Standing at the back of the church Tempe noted the majority of the mourners were the Cannatas' friends. She also spotted the neighbors from the cul-de-sac, old Mr. and Mrs. McKimson sat beside Yvette and Emory LaRue. Even Spence Gullott had turned up to pay his last respects. The work crew from the construction company was there too, accenting Tom's absence.

Crying openly as she finished the song, the soloist returned to her seat. Hutch, wearing his dark gray suit, stepped to the altar. Before he could speak, the door to the sanctuary opened and Tom stepped inside. Heads turned, eyes stared, mouths dropped open and people gasped.

Tom walked down the aisle with a woman on his arm. Tempe recognized her immediately—Annie Johnson. She had gone to high school with Tempe, but in those days she was Annie Kruziek. She'd become Johnson when she married her late wealthy husband. Along with the name change, Annie's appearance had undergone drastic alterations. Drab brown hair was now bright red. Cosmetic surgery had given her a pert nose and bigger eyes—and obviously, breast implants. If Tempe hadn't been around to note the changes, she wouldn't recognize Annie as her former classmate.

Like everyone else, she was startled to see Annie with Tom. Not only because it was inappropriate to bring his girlfriend to his wife's funeral but because Tempe hadn't known they were seeing each other. Obviously, Jackie hadn't been aware of it either.

As the couple hurried down the aisle, seeming to relish the stir they caused, Hutch said, a tad louder than necessary, "Please open your hymnals to page 125."

Though everyone quickly thumbed through the music books, furtive and disproving glances were thrown toward the couple. The organ's opening chords of "God Will Take Care of You," drowned out the whispers and rustling pages.

It was just as well Ronnie wasn't here.

Hutch continued the service smoothly, making Tempe wonder if Tom had warned him beforehand, but she dismissed the thought, knowing her husband would have convinced him of the inappropriateness of the action.

When the singing and eulogy were over, the crowd moved outside. Pallbearers carried the white casket out the side door and up the hillside of the cemetery. Pine, aspen, silver and valley oaks surrounded the grassy area. Hutch followed with Tom right behind with Annie leaning heavily on his arm. She was having trouble walking in her high heels on the soft ground. The other mourners trailed along, Tempe bringing up the rear.

After the casket was set in place next to the waiting grave, Hutch bowed his head. Tempe noticed movement behind a tall monument, and while Hutch pronounced a final, simple prayer commending Jackie's soul to the Lord's keeping, Tempe moved quickly.

Crouching low but intent upon the ritual before him, Ronnie didn't notice Tempe's approach. She grabbed his arm before he could get away. "Why didn't you come inside for the service?"

"Didn't want to be in the same room with Tom and his bimbo. Can you believe him? I ought to bash his face in."

"It wasn't good judgment on his part. Are you doing okay?"

He glanced toward the casket, tears in his eyes. "I thought I hated her. But now that she's gone..."

Tempe put her arm around Ronnie, and for a brief moment she felt his weight against her. "I know this is rough. Where are you staying, Ronnie? Maybe I can help you."

He jerked away. "Around. And I don't need any help."

"Fine, but I still have to know where I can find you."

Before he could answer, angry shouting drew her attention. The crowd parted to reveal Tom swinging at the taller, gaunt figure of Spence Gullott.

"Stay put, Ronnie!" Tempe admonished as she darted toward the fighting figures. By the time she reached them, Hutch had pulled Tom away, and Emory LaRue had a bear hug on a still flailing Gullott. If not for the disruption of the somber occasion, the sight of the much shorter and pudgier Emory containing the gaunt, crane-like Gullott would have been humorous.

"What is going on here?" Tempe asked.

Hutch released his hold on Tom, and the voluptuous Annie fluttered around him. "Oh, sweetheart, did that dreadful man hurt you?"

Tom ignored her and glared at the puffing Gullott. "What's the matter with you, man? Have you gone nuts or something?"

"Let me at him!" Gullott hollered, straining at the hold Emory had around his middle. "He's the one who ought to be in that casket!"

"Calm down, Spence," Tempe stood directly in front of him. "What's this all about?"

"The man's crazy," Tom said.

"If I am you made me that way," Gullott spat, the veins in his neck bulging. "Let me go, Emory, you're cutting off my air."

Emory peered around his skinny prisoner. "What do you say, Deputy?"

"Okay, turn him loose. But you better behave yourself, Spence, or I'll handcuff you."

Emory released Gullott but hovered nearby. Yvette clasped her husband's arm, smiling as though she enjoyed the spectacle.

"One of you tell me what happened here," Tempe ordered.

Glaring at Gullott, Tom said, "That idiot started it."

"All I did was tell Cannata now that he hasn't got a house he might as well drain that damn pond." Spence adjusted his glasses.

"And I told him this wasn't the time to be talking about it. Nothing has changed about my pond anyway. Then this nut case starts swinging on me. All I did was defend myself."

"Tom is right, Spence, Jackie's funeral isn't the place to be discussing the pond," Tempe said.

Spence folded his arms, eyes flashing beneath his overhanging brow. "It's the only chance I've had. The bum won't talk to me anywhere else."

"Since you can't seem to work this out any other way, you ought to seek legal advice," Tempe suggested.

"Fine idea." He pointed a long, knobby finger in Tom's direction. "I'll see you in court." Whirling, Spence pushed his way past those who had remained to watch the show.

Tom smirked. "Whatever. Can you believe that guy?"

"He's understandably upset about the pond. After all, if the dam bursts it will dump right on his house." Tempe glanced over to where she'd left Ronnie standing behind the monument. He was no longer there. "Did anyone see where Ronnie went?"

"He was here?" Tom seemed genuinely surprised. "He actually showed up for his mother's funeral?"

That wasn't any more shocking than Tom's appearance with a girlfriend on his arm but Tempe kept that comment to herself. "I really need to talk to Ronnie. If you should run into him, try convincing him to give me a call."

Tom snorted. "I doubt I'll see him and even if I do, I couldn't convince him to do anything."

"Ronnie told me you kept a gun in the bedroom. What kind, Tom?"

He sighed. "I suppose you'll find out one way or another. It was a .38, Smith and Wesson."

"Thanks." Before Tempe could think of another question, Yvonne waddled over.

"You're really looking fantastic, Annie."

"Why, thank you." Annie squinted at the pudgy woman. "Well, for goodness sake, it's you. Yvette Slader. Do you live in Bear Creek now?"

Yvette nodded and grinned knowingly at Tom. "Right across the way from Mr. Cannata's place. And my married name is LaRue."

Tom pulled on Annie's arm. "Come on, it's time to get out of here."

Annie teetered beside him on her high heels, her bright red mane poofing out behind her. She glanced back and waved her heavily ringed fingers at Yvette. "We'll have to get together sometime."

A vague remembrance flitted into Tempe's brain: the Annie Kruziek of old, mousy brown hair and ordinary figure, giggling arm-in-arm with a chubby Yvette Slader as they made their way down the high school corridor toward class. Annie and Yvette had been best friends in high school. Tempe wondered why they'd lost track of one another.

"Are you ready to go?" Hutch asked, bringing her back to the present.

"Oh, sure." She had to spend some time conjuring up the past. Her high school days hadn't been all that pleasant. Because of her Yanduchi ancestry, she'd often been made fun of and called "half-breed" and "redskin". She'd successfully put aside those painful memories and, along with them, almost everything about her days at Dennison High. Perhaps Doretha could help her with remembering the past.

"Why do I have the impression you're off somewhere?"

She smiled at him. "Believe it or not, I was thinking about high school."

He squeezed her around the waist. "I always thought you were the most beautiful girl on campus."

He'd told her that before. Hutch had been a couple of grades ahead of her and she didn't remember much about him except for his unruly auburn hair and freckles.

"You were the only one who thought that."

"I was the only one with any sense." He winked at her. "Let's go to lunch."

☙☙

Tempe forced herself not to talk about the case while they enjoyed their food in The Cafe. When they arrived back home she was glad that no one had left a message on the answering machine. "I have to call the Sergeant and let him know what I found out about the gun."

While she used the telephone, Hutch sorted through the mail. He frowned. "What do you suppose this is? Looks like an invitation of some sort." He dropped it on the table.

She glanced at the square envelope with bold printing on the front. No return address.

Sergeant Guthrie came on the line and Tempe gave him her full attention, telling him what Tom had said about his gun.

"Humph. Hasn't turned up in the ashes yet."

"Ronnie Keplinger made an appearance at the cemetery."

"Great! When are you bringing him in?"

"I'm not. He disappeared."

"What do you mean he disappeared?"

"Tom Cannata and Spence Gullott got into a fight and I had to break it up. Once I got them settled down, Ronnie was gone."

"You better find that kid and bring him in," the Sergeant growled.

"I'm sure he's staying somewhere in Bear Creek. It's just a matter of time before I run into him again."

Guthrie grumbled something about "priorities" and "the detectives" and hung up.

Tempe grinned at Hutch. "He's not too happy with me."

"He ought to be, considering how you've worked on your days off."

Tempe absently picked up the envelope and opened it. She drew out the single sheet of paper with words cut from the newspaper pasted on it.

"What on earth is that?" Hutch asked, reading over her shoulder. "'FOR YOUR HEALTH DON'T POKE YOUR NOSE INTO OTHER PEOPLE'S BUSINESS!' What is that supposed to mean?"

Tempe tossed it back on the table. "Who knows? There's a nut case loose, I suppose."

"Wait a minute, Tempe, you might be in danger. I'd better cancel my trip."

Tempe was glad she hadn't told him about the similar phone messages she'd received earlier. "Don't be silly, darling. You've been looking forward to this conference too long to change your plans for something as stupid as an anonymous letter. I'm not worried about it. You certainly don't have to be."

"I want you to call the Sergeant back and let him know about this right now."

"Tell you what, why don't I run it down to the substation? I've got a couple of things I need to do in town anyway unless you need some help with your packing."

"I can handle my packing, but I'm still not sure I should leave you."

Tempe smoothed his freckled cheek. "Of course you're going. I'll be fine, and Blair will be here. Truly, sweetheart, there's nothing to worry about."

"You talk to the Sergeant, see what he says. If he thinks I should stay home, I will."

Tempe held his face in her hands and kissed his lips. "I love you. Now get ready for your big weekend."

⚜ ⚜

Dennison wasn't Tempe's primary destination. She wanted to drop by Spence Gullott's and ask him a few more questions—including his whereabouts when Jackie was murdered. The Gullott home was situated in a secluded vale. Behind the modern redwood structure, with lots of angles and glass, a sloping hill rose to a high dirt berm. Tempe knew that was the dam for Tom's pond. No wonder Spence was nervous.

A rustic wooden fence circled the yard. Children's voices rang out and the splashing sounds suggested they were playing in a pool. She followed the flagstone path to the large front door decorated with a multi-colored stained glass window.

Spence answered the loud door chimes. He was barefoot and wore only baggy shorts. A towel was draped around his neck. "Oh ... it's you." He didn't look pleased to see her.

"I have a few more questions for you."

"I'm busy right now. My wife and I are swimming with the children. I try to spend some time every day with my family. I work nights."

"This won't take long."

Sighing, he stepped aside so she could enter the cool interior.

The marble-floored entry opened into a huge great room with a stone fireplace. Colorful afghans and pillows embellished comfortable looking overstuffed couches and chairs. Toys were scattered on a sculpted pale green carpet. Glass doors opened onto a covered patio and bright furniture. Two small children floating in rings and a chubby, curly-haired woman were in the blue water of the oval pool beyond.

"That's my wife, Maureen and our kids." Spence gestured toward the pool but didn't lead her outside or invite her to sit down. His eyes bulged and seemed out of focus.

Tempe guessed it was because he wasn't wearing his glasses. "You have a nice family."

"I'd like to get back to them. What is it you want from me?" His tone was impatient.

"What was that ruckus about at the funeral?"

Spence's face reddened. "That man has a knack for raising my ire. Anyway, he hit me first." He cleared his throat. "It isn't necessary for you to mention what happened to my wife, is it? She abhors violence, and she didn't want me to go to the funeral."

"What I really came to find out is, what were you doing the night Jackie Cannata died?"

"What I'm always doing in the evening hours, working in my office."

"Can anyone verify that? Your wife perhaps?"

"She was here and knows my routine, if that's what you mean."

"I'd like to talk to her, Spence."

"Oh, for crying out loud. Why on earth are you making such a big deal out of this? I didn't shoot Mrs. Cannata or set her house on fire!"

"I'd like to be sure about that."

Through the glass door Tempe saw that Maureen Gullott and the children, a boy about five and girl around three, were out of the pool. She was toweling them off.

"I can't stand Tom Cannata. I haven't made a secret of that. He either bribed the building inspector or the man's an idiot to allow that pond to be constructed. If Tom were the one who was killed you'd have reason to come after me."

"You could have made a mistake and expected Tom to be there with his wife."

"Oh, come on, Deputy, give me some credit for brains."

Maureen and the children disappeared from view. Tempe guessed they'd entered through another door.

"Let me tell you what's bothering me," Tempe offered.

"Please do."

"When I talked to you the morning after the fire, you mentioned that Jackie had been shot. How did you know?"

Spence frowned. "Read it in the paper, I guess."

"No. There was nothing about the murder in the Fresno paper until the next morning. And of course Dennison's paper doesn't come out until afternoon."

He swiped back his hair. "I don't remember how I found out. Someone told me I suppose. I did not kill her, Deputy Crabtree!"

Maureen entered the room from a door near the fireplace. She wore a short, terry cloth robe, her hair wet and in tight ringlets. "Goodness, Spence, why didn't you ask the deputy to sit down? And offer her something to drink?" She handed him his glasses.

He shoved them on and glared through the thick lenses. "Because she's accusing me of murdering Jackie Cannata!"

Gasping, Maureen's hand flew to her pale lips. "Oh, that isn't possible."

"I haven't accused your husband of anything," Tempe said quietly. "I merely want to know what he was doing Monday evening."

Maureen tucked her arm through Spence's and gazed up at him. "You were working, weren't you?"

"Of course."

"Well, honey, I know you went into your office to work. I have no way of knowing whether you stayed there. After all, our bedroom is on the other side of the house."

"Maureen!" Spence pulled his arm from his wife's grasp.

"Don't get all upset. Never on this earth would I suspect you of doing harm to anyone and I'm sure Deputy Crabtree doesn't either. But I'm not going to lie. I was in our bedroom with the TV on, like every single evening. I have no way of knowing what Spence was up to."

"What are you trying to do to me, Maureen?"

"I'm not trying to do anything. I'm just stating a fact. You never come to bed until I'm asleep. How on earth could I possibly know if you're in the office or out gallivanting somewhere?"

Spence's face turned crimson. "Maureen!"

His wife lifted her round chin. "I'm merely speaking the truth."

"You know I don't go 'gallivanting', as you put it," Spence said loudly.

Maureen shrugged but didn't look at him. "I only know that you don't come to bed until after I'm long asleep."

Spence took a step backward. "I'm working hard to provide you and the kids with everything you need and want!"

"Not everything I need or want." Maureen held her arms out to him, but he ignored the gesture.

Tempe raised her hands. "I think you folks need to sit down and talk about this." Tempe was as surprised by Maureen's revelation as Spence seemed to be.

"She isn't being fair, Deputy. She knows how upset I've been about that stupid pond!"

Remembering the fight at the cemetery, Tempe nodded. "Your

husband is certainly concerned about it."

"Obsessed is the word! That's what he is about everything, ob- sessed."

"Can't you talk some sense into her, Deputy? My family's safety is my primary concern."

Maureen turned to him. Hands on her hips, she faced Spence, defiantly. "You better make me your primary concern, or you won't have a family to worry about."

CHAPTER 11

Apparently Spence expected Tempe to come up with the solution to his marital problems. She stayed long enough to suggest if he and his wife couldn't discuss their differences amicably, perhaps they ought to seek the help of a marriage counselor. Though Tempe hadn't thought Spence the type to solve his problems with violence, his actions at the funeral made her wonder. His concern about the pond might have pushed him over the edge—something to consider.

Tempe found Sergeant Guthrie in his office and immediately began her explanation of why Spence Gullott should be counted as one of the suspects in Jackie's murder. "He could have taken out his anger with Tom on Jackie. He doesn't have a good explanation for the time, and he knew Jackie had been shot before it was announced to the public."

"So you think this Gullott character murdered Mrs. Cannata?"

Shrugging, Tempe said, "It's possible, but her husband still seems more likely. Someone ought to investigate Spence, just in case. After all, he doesn't have an alibi."

"I'll mention him to the detectives, but they seem to be leaning toward the son. It would certainly help if you would make a concentrated effort to bring him in." He stared at her.

"I will as soon as I find him."

Guthrie picked up a fat folder from a stack of many. "Is that all?"

"One more thing." She dropped the square envelope with the block printing onto his desk.

"What's this?" The Sergeant pulled out the single sheet of paper and read the pasted-on words. "When did you get this?"

"Came in today's mail. And threatening messages have been left on our answering machine."

"You think this person is trying to get you to stay away from the

Cannata murder?"

Tempe raised her eyebrows and lifted her hands, palms upward. "What else could it be?"

"Whoever it is must be stupid. The case is being investigated by detectives. Even if you do stay out of it, and you should, the guilty party will be apprehended."

Nodding, Tempe thought for a moment. "Unless there's something important that only I know about."

"Like what?"

"I don't have a clue."

Guthrie tossed the note aside. "I doubt there's anything to worry about. Most likely it's the handiwork of some crank."

"That's what I told my husband."

"Once you find that kid, you won't have any reason to be involved. You can handle him, can't you?"

"Of course."

✧✧

Tempe arrived home the same time Blair drove up in his yellow Volkswagen bug. "Hi, Mom," he greeted, unfolding his long body from the tiny car.

"Hi, sweetie. Have you seen Ronnie lately?"

"Keplinger?"

She nodded.

"Nope."

"Do me a favor and ask around, will you? I'm supposed to take him in for questioning."

Blair opened the back door for her. "What for? You don't think he killed his mother, do you?"

"I don't really know. I didn't think, so but his disappearing makes him look suspicious."

"He's such a flake. There's no telling what's going on in his mind." Blair headed for the refrigerator, always his first stop when he came home from school.

"There's one more thing I'd like to run by you."

He put a carton of milk on the table and the rest of the berry cobbler left from dinner. "What's that?"

"I got a threatening phone call on the answering machine. Have you noticed anything unusual lately? Like someone calling and hanging up?"

Beneath his corn silk hair, his forehead furrowed. "What do you mean, 'threatening'? Someone wants to hurt you?"

"It wasn't specific. The message was, 'Keep your nose out of other people's business or you'll be sorry.'"

Blair dropped into the chair. "Who was it?"

"I couldn't tell."

"A man or a woman?"

"The voice was disguised. Could have been either."

"That sounds like something Ronnie might do."

"What about a letter?"

"You got a letter too?"

She described it and the message.

"Oh man. If Keplinger did that, I'll beat the crap out of him."

"That won't help."

"But he won't threaten you ever again when I get through with him."

"I don't know if Ronnie is responsible, but I do need to locate him. That's how you can be the most helpful to me. I know you'll be working at the fire station all weekend. Keep an eye out for him. Ask around if any of the other firemen have seen him."

"Yeah. Well, if I do find out he's the one..."

"Eat your cobbler."

He wiggled his forefinger at her. "I want you to be careful, Mom. If you see anyone, or anything suspicious, don't mess around. Call for backup right away."

She leaned down and kissed his forehead.

When Tempe stopped at home for her dinner break, both Hutch and Blair were present, though Blair had already eaten. While Hutch put their food on the table, Tempe asked her son, "Did you find out anything about Ronnie? Did anyone see him or have any idea where he might be staying?"

"No, sorry. But I did tell everyone to be watching for him."

"Thanks, honey. He's bound to turn up soon."

Blair went to his room to study for a final. Tempe and Hutch sat down and dished up their food.

"Are you all packed?" Tempe asked Hutch.

"Yes, I am, but I still feel uneasy about leaving you."

"Oh, sweetheart, go on and have a wonderful time. I'll have my hands full all weekend."

Hutch nodded and began eating. "Have you been busy this evening?"

"Nope. Actually it's very quiet. The lull before the storm, as they say."

They visited congenially until Tempe had to return to work. Kissing her at the door, Hutch said, "I'll be going early tomorrow morning."

"Be sure and wake me to say goodbye."

Though Hutch still seemed reluctant about the trip, Tempe felt sure he wouldn't change his plans, and she could meet Doretha as she'd promised.

Throughout the rest of her shift, she made several passes by the park hoping to see the glow of a cigarette tip, signaling Ronnie's presence. She was disappointed. Of course, if he were trying to avoid her—and he probably was—he wouldn't hang around the park.

Hutch left before daybreak Friday morning. Tempe didn't go on duty until her usual four p.m., but she heard from the dispatcher several times. All the campgrounds were full. Overnight, the call-volume increased. The tourist season had begun and extra deputies were assigned to Tempe's patrol area.

She investigated one noisy party complaint after another. After ten, she received a call about a live band playing loudly and disturbing neighbors. She located a huge gathering of young adults outside a large barn on one of the ranches. The musicians' speakers were turned up full blast and the sound echoed from the surrounding hills. "Either turn down the volume or stop the music," she ordered.

She glanced at her watch. Not too much longer and she'd find out what Doretha had planned for her.

On her way back over the winding road, she slowed at an abandoned house she'd passed many times before. The yard was overgrown with weeds. Some windows were boarded-up, others broken. She noticed a flicker of light, and started to pull over, but the radio crackled to life. The dispatcher sent her to a rollover accident.

She spent the remainder of her shift speeding from one incident to another. With extra deputies and highway patrol on duty, she was able to quit working at the proper time. Excited and a bit apprehensive about what was coming, she headed toward the reservation.

She saw Doretha outlined in the open door when she parked in front of the house. Though much shorter than Tempe, the shaman's demeanor always made her seem taller than she actually was. "Ah," she greeted, "You were able to get away earlier than you expected." She wore a simple deerskin gown with fringed sleeves and hem.

Awed, Tempe nodded, and followed Doretha inside. Only moonlight flooded through the open French doors. The air was heavy with the scent of herbs with a floral undertone.

"I have something for you to change into," Doretha said. "You'll find it in the room at the top of the stairs."

A lamp was on in a small study. A gown similar to the one Doretha wore lay on a cow-skin couch. Tempe quickly removed her utility belt and holster, placing them on the chair beside a desk. She took off her uniform and draped it on a coat tree. She fingered the supple softness of the simple Indian dress before slipping it over her head. She exchanged her boots for a pair of leather moccasins she found on the floor. Unclipping her barrette, she let her braid hang down her back, glimpsing herself in an oval mirror hanging over the desk. She smiled, thinking how much she resembled her Yanduchi grandmother.

Doretha made no mention of Tempe's transformation. "Come. Follow me," she said.

CHAPTER 12

Doretha led the way through the rear yard surrounded by oaks and cottonwoods. Flowers and herbs grew in profusion, their scent much stronger than it had been inside. Bathed in moonlit iridescence, a narrow path snaked its way toward the rocky hillside. Though she couldn't see the nearby river, Tempe heard it singing over its rocky bed.

Moving quickly and silently, Doretha headed upward. When Tempe was nearly out of breath, Doretha halted. They reached the summit of the first of many hills, one behind the other, becoming higher and more formidable, finally blending into a barricade of rugged mountains. This first crest was to be the setting for the forthcoming ritual. A small drum, rattles, and a string of bells were arranged on a straw mat along with a large abalone shell, several smudge sticks and matches.

The moon cast a silvery glow on their surroundings. Doretha extended her arms and lifted her face. "When the moon is full, the Great Spirit casts his eternal light on the world."

Misgivings nudged Tempe, but she pushed them from her mind.

"First we will purify ourselves." Doretha lit one of the smudge sticks and let it burn in the abalone shell. She lifted the shell and moved it around Tempe's body as if to bathe her in the smoke. Tempe recognized the scent—sage and sweet grass.

"This will cleanse the frustrations and negative thoughts and emotions from your mind and soul."

The smoke swirled around Tempe. Doretha lit a second stick in the shell and moved it around herself. The sweet, pungent odor filled the night air.

"This will make it possible for us to walk in balance and harmony."

She moved the abalone shell up and down to spiral the smoke

around them.

Exchanging the shell for the drum, Doretha began to beat out a rhythm with her hands. "Dance like grass in the wind."

Though Tempe had only danced to the drum twice before, she didn't hesitate. She lifted and touched down her moccasined feet with the drumbeat, swaying back and forth. In time she realized that her own breathing and heart pulsed in the same cadence, the phenomena she'd experienced the other times.

"The drum puts us in touch with our inner spirit. It will free us from our earthly bonds," Doretha explained. She continued to beat the drum while Tempe danced.

Sense of time left Tempe. She had no idea how long she danced in the moonlight on top of the hill behind Doretha's house.

All at once she was aware the drum had stopped.

"I want you to lie down on the mat and relax. Look at the stars," Doretha directed.

Tempe did as she was told. The sky was ablaze with bright and twinkling stars. She was no longer aware of anything but the vastness of the universe and her soul.

"Pick out a particular star. Focus on it."

Overhead, one seemed even brighter than all the rest. Tempe stared at it. It winked acknowledgment.

"Feel the starlight enter your body through your eyes. Breathe deeply. Allow the starlight to fill you completely."

Tempe could actually feel the cool brilliance penetrate her being, swelling, making her full.

"Your awareness will expand with light."

As Doretha spoke, she began shaking the rattle and the bells.

"All tensions disappear."

Jingle, jingle. Ka-chuck, ka-chuck, ka-chuck.

Though Doretha continued to speak, jingle the bells, and shake the rattle, the words, the jingling, the ka-chuck all ran together.

"... Mystical ... "

Ching, ching, ching.

" ... Sacred powers ... "

Ka-chuck, ka-chuck.

" ... Earth spirit ... "

Ching, ching.

The star grew brighter.

" ... vibrations of the words ... "

Ching, ching, ching.

Ka-chuck, ka-chuck.

A trace of sage smoke lingered in the air.

" ... awareness expanding ... "

Finally, the words and the jingling of the bells and the shaking of the rattle blended together until, like the scent of the smoke, they disappeared into the night.

Tempe opened her eyes. The stars had faded and the sky was pale pewter. She'd spent the whole night on the hilltop. Pulling herself into a sitting position, she glanced around. Doretha was gone, as were the trappings of the starlight ritual. Despite sleeping on the ground, Tempe felt refreshed.

While she thought about what had transpired the night before, as unusual as it had been, she was disappointed. She'd expected something spectacular, a vision perhaps.

"Oh, well." She scrambled to her feet, and dusted off the Indian gown, feeling oddly out-of-place.

Hurrying down the hill, she was anxious to get into her own, more familiar clothing. Doretha was not in the living room, nor did Tempe hear stirring elsewhere in the house. But as she started up the staircase, she found a folded piece of gray stationery with Tempe written in large circular letters. Inside was only one sentence. "The only limits are those we impose upon ourselves."

What did that mean?

CHAPTER 13

Back home, Tempe was once greeted by an empty house, a note, and a blinking answering machine. She read the note. It was from Blair and no surprise. If she needed him, he could be reached at the fire station.

She pushed the button on the machine. The first message was from Hutch, letting her know he'd arrived at his destination and giving her the phone number where he could be reached.

The second message was from the disguised voice. For a moment, Tempe felt a tickle of recognition as it spewed a venomous string of obscenities followed by, "Drop your investigation, Deputy, or you'll be sorry!"

Tempe shook her head, rewound the tape and listened to it again. There was something familiar about the voice right at the beginning, but she couldn't put a name to it. Except for Ronnie, she hadn't heard anyone spouting such foul language recently. But it didn't sound like Ronnie. Of course, despite something she couldn't put her finger on, it really didn't sound like anyone else she knew either. Was she letting the fact that she didn't want Ronnie to be guilty influence her judgment?

She spent the remainder of the day doing household chores and fixing a casserole she and Blair could easily heat when they found time to come home. At four o'clock, dressed in her sharply pressed, khaki uniform, Tempe backed the Blazer out of the driveway, ready to begin her evening's work.

The highway was alive with all types of vehicles traveling into and out of the mountains. The parking lots of all of Bear Creek's businesses were filled. Good for the local economy. Driving to the lake, Tempe cruised through the campground. All the sites were occupied, fires flickered here and there. Checking with the ranger, Tempe learned that so far, all campers were congenial and adhering to the rules.

As the evening progressed, she handed out a couple of speeding tickets, was first to respond to the scene of a non-injury accident, gave out directions to various places, and investigated the theft of the contents of a car left unlocked while the occupants were skinny-dipping in the river. All the while, she watched for Ronnie but didn't see him.

After midnight, she decided to drive past the abandoned house she'd noticed the night before. A faint light came from one of the back windows. Tempe parked the Blazer in the weed-choked driveway.

Moonlight filtering through the trees and bushes cast eerie shadows on the one-story structure. Tempe turned on the flashlight as she remembered Doretha's warning. This would certainly be the time and place for something bad to happen.

The history of the house was mysterious. At one time, it had been the home of a pioneer ranch family who owned several hundred surrounding acres. The next property owner built another, more luxurious house on the other side of the hill, for a time using the first for guests or the employees of the ranch. A long standing rumor held that it was the site of the unexplained death of a young woman and her ghost lingered on. Whether or not the reputation for being haunted was the cause, the house had been abandoned long ago and left in disrepair. Over the years it had been occupied off-and-on by various down-and-outers seeking shelter. Tempe suspected Ronnie fell into that category.

She made her approach cautiously, no telling who she might discover. She carried her flashlight, but the bright moonlight made turning it on unnecessary. However, it could serve as a weapon if needed.

A narrow path was visible through the weeds, flattened by feet that had traipsed through previously, leading to a sagging porch. A broken lattice shielded the side entrance. The first step creaked loudly when Tempe stepped onto it. She paused and listened.

An owl hooted. A breeze rustled the leaves in a nearby sycamore, but she heard nothing from inside.

She took another step. Again, a board creaked. Switching on the flashlight, Tempe shoved the door open. She swept the entrance with the light beam. "Ronnie! Ronnie Keplinger! Are you here?" An old couch spilled its filling. A broken, chair rested on its side. Trash was scattered over the battered and warped floor. Most windows were covered with boards, and a door hanging on one hinge led into a hall. An archway opened into what once might have been the dining room.

"What? Who's there?" A voice hollered back.

"It's Deputy Crabtree. Come on out here where I can see you."

Heavy footsteps approached and Ronnie stepped into the doorway. "How did you find me?" he growled. He was dressed in his usual olive and brown camouflage fatigues.

"Not much gets past me." She took a step nearer. "You know I've been wanting to talk to you. Why did you disappear at the cemetery?"

"Maybe I didn't want to talk to you." He crossed his arms and leaned against the broken door.

"It will be a lot easier to answer my questions than the detectives'. And eventually you will have to account for your time on the night your mother was killed."

"Well, what if I can't?"

"Listen to me, Ronnie. You're one of the suspects in your mother's murder."

"That's stupid! I didn't like my mother very much, but I wouldn't kill her."

"I don't think you did, but you're going to have to explain to the detectives what you were doing that night." Tempe moved closer to him, keeping her eyes fixed on his face.

He ran his hand over his closely cropped hair. "Oh, man. I don't even like to think about it."

"You know if you would just explain it to them, then eventually everyone would leave you alone."

"People aren't ever going to leave me alone."

He might be right. "Let's take this one step at a time, Ronnie. You told me you had a fight with your mother and that's why you left. Where did you go?"

"I came here. I've kept a sleeping bag and some supplies here for a while. I've been using this place as a hangout."

"Anyone else know you've been here?"

He shook his head. "But deputy, I just told you, a bunch of my stuff is here. That ought to prove something."

Unfortunately, because Ronnie had carted some of his belongings to the old house ahead of time, it might look to Detective Morrison that Ronnie had premeditated the murder and the fire.

"Ronnie, I want to help you. If I don't take you in to talk to the detectives, they're going to come after you. It would look a lot better if you cooperated with me, and them."

"I suppose none of you will be satisfied until you've done this."

"That's right, Ronnie." Tempe smiled. "Why don't you come with me now and spend the night at my place? You could take a shower, have something to eat. You'll have to sleep on the couch, but that might be a bit more comfortable than the floor."

Ronnie shook his head. "No, I don't want to do that."

"Why not?"

"I'm fine here."

"I don't want to take you in tonight. You'd have to spend the night in jail." Maybe even more, depending upon what the detectives thought after they questioned him. "But Ronnie, I don't want you to disappear again. I must know that I can find you when I'm ready to take you to the substation."

"I don't have anyplace else to go. I'll be here."

"Can I count on you to keep your word this time?" She searched his face hoping for some inkling of his true feeling. It was crazy for her to trust him. No, she had to take him.

He must have guessed what she'd decided because he said, quickly, "If you'll wait until tomorrow, I'll tell you something you don't know about my mother's murder."

"Why don't you tell me now?" Tempe asked.

"No, I don't want to. That's what I'm using to bargain with."

Leaving him there went against her better judgment. If he did know something that could help solve the case, maybe it would be worth taking the chance. "Okay, Ronnie. Don't disappoint me."

She glanced at her watch. It was almost time for her shift to end.

His arms crossed, Ronnie leaned against the door jamb. "When will you be back?"

"I'm not sure. Maybe tomorrow. I'll call my Sergeant and talk to him and see what he wants. He might want to wait until Monday. We'll see."

"You don't expect me to stick around here all the time, do you?"

"If I don't show up by ten, you can do whatever you want just so long as you stay around Bear Creek."

"Where am I supposed to go? I don't have any wheels."

That wouldn't stop him, if he really wanted to leave. Though she didn't have any reason to trust him, she continued to believe in his innocence. "If I don't come tomorrow, I'll be here bright and early on Monday."

He turned on the heels of his boots and disappeared into the darkness beyond the door.

"Hope I'm right about you."

She headed back to the Blazer. Clouds scudded across the moon and Tempe left her flashlight on to brighten her way. Uneasiness fell over her, and she turned to look back at the house, half expecting to see Ronnie charging at her with a weapon. But no one was there. All these warnings and threats were getting to her.

Inside the Blazer, she glanced in her rearview mirror before driving away. Down the road, a vehicle without its lights on, made a sudden turn, vanishing around the bend. What was that about? Just as she put her hands on the wheel ready to whip around and follow, a call came over the radio.

"CHP needs assistance," the dispatcher snapped. The location was about a mile down the highway. Tempe arrived there in minutes.

"Oh, dear," she groaned, immediately recognizing Spence Gullott's red Suburban parked in front of a black-and-white highway patrol unit. Spence gestured wildly before the CHP officer, legs braced apart, hands on hips.

She pulled in behind the black-and-white and got out. The officer was spewing a deluge of words. Approaching, she said, "I'm Deputy Crabtree, how can I be of assistance? Hi, Spence."

The CHP officer slid his glasses down and peered over them at her. "You know this turkey?"

"Yes, I'm acquainted with Mr. Gullott. What's the problem?"

"I don't know what's the matter," Spence hollered, "This yahoo stopped me for no reason."

"Let's not call each other names," Tempe said, looking from Spence to the CHP officer, hoping he, as well as Gullott, would follow her advice.

"Ha! 'No reason', he says. This guy was all over the road. When I asked to see his license, he jumped out of the car and started bouncing around like some kind of nut case. I'm ready to take him in."

"Why don't you show the officer your driver's license, Spence?"

Tempe said quietly.

"That's the problem." Spence thrashed his arms. "I left home without my wallet."

Sneering, the CHP officer said, "He's drunk or on drugs."

"I'm not drunk!" Spence shouted. Tempe heard a slur in his words and his eyes were too bright.

Tempe moved nearer. "Do you have a problem, Spence?"

"Oh, yeah, I've got a problem all right. And I've got you to thank for it." He ran both hands through his hair as he paced back and forth in front of her.

"Don't get too close, Deputy. This guy may be dangerous." The CHP unsnapped his holster.

Tempe waved her hand at him. "It's okay." She planted herself in front of Spence. "Talk to me, Spence. What is it you think I've done?"

He seemed to be having trouble focusing. "You got my wife all riled up when you came to see us. She hasn't been acting right since. She's demanding that I come to bed early. She bought some sleeping pills and made me take them. But they don't make me sleepy. They have the opposite effect. I can't be still. I thought maybe if I went for a drive..."

"Oh, sure," the CHP said. "It's the medication that made him drive that way. If you believe that, you'll believe anything."

"Damn. It's the truth." Something must have snapped inside Spence because he balled up his fist and swung on the officer, connecting. The CHP officer's breath came out in a wheeze as he fell over backwards.

Spence's mouth dropped open.

"Now you've done it," Tempe said, reaching for him.

He jerked away, and darted toward his Suburban.

Tempe leaped after him, crashing against him with such force she knocked him to the ground. Straddling his legs, she pulled his arms behind him and fastened her handcuffs around his wrists.

"That was a big mistake, Spence," she said, scrambling to her feet.

The highway patrolman stood, rubbing his chin and rotating his jaw. "I didn't expect that. Thanks for corralling him, Deputy. I'll take over now." He grabbed Spence's arm and yanked him up. "You're under arrest for assaulting an officer. You have the right to remain silent... "

Tempe shook her head. She waited until the officer put the loudly protesting Spence in the back seat of his car. "He really isn't acting like himself, Officer. I think he was probably telling the truth about the medication."

"Doesn't make any difference, the guy attacked me without provocation."

"I'm not excusing him for what he did. But I am suggesting that you might take him by the hospital before you book him and have them draw some blood."

"You may be right," he conceded. "You want to call for a tow truck?"

"I'll take care of his vehicle." She planned to let Maureen Gullott know what happened, to hear what she had to say about the sleeping pills, and Spence's reaction to them, letting her collect the Suburban when she could. She took the keys from the ignition, pocketed them, and pushed the lock button on the driver's door.

The CHP unit pulled away from the curb. Tempe's last glimpse of Spence was of his mouth, dark and moving in his long, gaunt face, no doubt vehemently protesting his arrest. Spence was eccentric even without the adverse reaction to the sleeping pill. He'd become violent with Tom Cannata, and now with the highway patrolman. Perhaps Gullott lost control Monday night, burst into Cannatas' house looking for Tom, confronted Jackie and shot her. Then setting a fire to cover up.

Tempe had trouble accepting that possibility, but she never expected to see Spence get physically violent either, and she'd witnessed that twice. Though tomorrow was Sunday, she needed to call Sergeant Guthrie and bring him up-to-date.

A flash of remembrance struck Tempe. She was at one end of the long corridor at the high school, Annie and Yvette carrying their books, giggling and whispering to each other, were at the other. A large group of girls approached them, but then the memory faded. Why did she remember that now?

CHAPTER 14

Tempe could hear the irritation in Sergeant Guthrie's voice because she'd called him at home on a Sunday. "I thought you'd want to know what happened with Spence Gullott," she said after describing the man's erratic behavior and subsequent arrest. "I talked to his wife and she corroborated his explanation about the sleeping pills. Said they made him hyper."

"Is that all?" The sergeant asked.

"Not exactly." She quickly told him about her encounter with Ronnie in the abandoned house.

"Quit fooling around with that kid, Crabtree. I want you to bring him in today. No more excuses," Sergeant Guthrie snapped. She knew he was angry because she hadn't brought Ronnie into the station any of the times she'd seen him despite orders to do so. She couldn't help wondering about her own motivations.

Tempe hated to take him in because she didn't think he'd killed his mother. As far as she knew there wasn't any evidence to prove that he had either. Her hunch was that Detective Morrison counted on bullying Ronnie into confessing. Besides, Ronnie had promised to disclose information about his mother's death and Tempe wanted to hear what it was. But arguing with the Sergeant wouldn't change the situation and would only make him angrier at her than he already was.

"Okay, I'll bring him in."

"You just better hope that he's where you left him, Crabtree."

"He promised he'd be there."

"He better be." The Sergeant hung up the phone.

Blair came in the kitchen wearing his Bear Creek Fire Department uniform. He grinned sheepishly. "Thought since Hutch was gone, I'd skip church today."

Tempe sighed. "Well, I'm not going to be there either. The Sergeant says I have to pick up Ronnie and take him down to the station for questioning."

"Probably a good idea if he's the one who's been harassing you." Blair pulled a box of cereal out of the cupboard.

"If you'd like, I can cook you some breakfast."

"Naw, that's okay."

"Hutch will be disappointed we didn't listen to his substitute preacher." Tempe took a bowl from the cupboard and poured cereal and milk into it. Might as well eat something before she put on her uniform and went after Ronnie.

"I'm gonna tell Hutch that I didn't want to hear anyone else."

Tempe laughed. "I don't think that will work. He knows how you feel about volunteering at the fire department. But I do have to follow my bosses' orders."

"That'll be a first," Blair teased.

Tempe chose to ignore the remark. "Tell me about school. What are your plans for grad night?"

"I'm going to be working at the fire station. If any of my classmates get stupid and have an accident, I want to be there to help out."

"Couldn't you take one night off and have some fun?"

"Mom, that is fun."

She shook her head. She'd set the example, making her work the most important thing in her life, what did she expect? She asked him more questions about school, what finals he had coming up, how he felt he would do as far as his grades, what his friends' plans were.

After he left, she tidied up the kitchen before she showered and changed into her uniform. She had plenty of time before the ten o'clock deadline she'd given Ronnie. As she worked, she considered her ambivalent feelings about him. Perhaps they were somehow tangled with her guilt about raising Blair. She always felt like she'd never spent enough time with him. Yet, he turned out all right despite it.

Poor Ronnie, living in a home besieged by domestic violence must've been like living in a war zone. No wonder he was so angry.

❧❧

In bright daylight, the old house no longer looked menacing, only dilapidated and forlorn. Tempe parked and made her way down the pathway through the weeds.

When she reached the door, she pounded on it and hollered, "Hey,

Ronnie. It's me, Deputy Crabtree."

There was no answer.

She shoved the door open. "Ronnie." Stepping inside, the dismal interior seemed unnaturally quiet. Cobwebs draped the corners and hung from the ceiling. She began to fear the worst. He'd betrayed her trust.

Maybe he'd only left to eat. If his sleeping bag and belongings were in the other room, she'd know he intended to return and keep his promise.

The house was bigger than it looked from the outside. Besides the dining room and kitchen off the living room, a long hall separated four bedrooms, two on each side. Tempe found the one Ronnie had been sleeping in. She could tell by the boot marks in the thick layer of dust, along with the discarded chip bags and candy wrappers. Nothing else of his was there.

"Darn." She shouldn't have trusted him after all. Oh, boy. Sergeant Guthrie was really going to be angry. Since it was Sunday, she wouldn't have to call him yet. Perhaps she'd be able to locate Ronnie before the end of the day.

She ought to go look for him but didn't have a clue where to begin. If he had friends, she didn't know who they were. Where could he be? Better start with likely places nearby.

Tempe drove up and down the country roads, searching for abandoned structures within walking distance. She searched through a disintegrating shed and a nearly collapsed barn to no-avail. When she'd looked everywhere she could think of, she decided to give up for a while. Maybe she'd run into him later in the day. She stopped at the fire station and asked Blair and the other volunteers to let her know if any of them spotted Ronnie.

Though she wasn't supposed to be working yet, she was already in uniform so she stopped wherever she saw anyone and asked if they'd seen Ronnie. Not having any luck, she finally gave up and returned home. The light was blinking on the answering machine.

The first message was from Hutch. "Sorry I missed you, sweetheart. Just wanted to let you know that I'll get home sometime tomorrow afternoon. Hope you're being careful. I love you."

She opened the refrigerator, looking for something to fix for lunch.

The answering machine continued to play. "You don't listen, do you?" It was that ugly, disguised, growling voice. "Something bad is going to happen to you if you don't keep your nose out of other people's business. This is your last warning!"

Oh, crap. It must be Ronnie threatening her. She sighed. Maybe she'd been wrong about him all along. She'd put too much reliance on her instincts and the hope that somehow she'd attained at least a bit of spiritual wisdom through Doretha's starlight ritual.

Until time to go on duty, Tempe remained at home. She tried to do some paperwork, but her mind kept going back to Ronnie. She found it so difficult to believe that he was responsible for his mother's death. But why would he run away like that and leave threatening messages on her answering machine if he was innocent?

❧❧

Back on duty that evening, when it was nearly eleven, the dispatcher sent Tempe to an affluent neighborhood. Most of the homes were surrounded by at least two acres. She easily found the address she was looking for. The number and the names Dr. and Mrs. Petrie were stenciled on the mailbox at the bottom of the hill. Tempe knew he was a pediatrician with a practice in Dennison. She drove up the winding driveway to the sprawling house.

Mrs. Petrie stood near the front door. She was in her late forties, her short brunette curls shot with silver. When Tempe climbed out of the Blazer, she hurried toward her, her plain face showing distress. "I'm sorry to bother you like this. If Daniel were here, I'd send him over to investigate. But he had an emergency tonight and had to go to the hospital. Of course, you don't need to know that."

"What's the problem, Mrs. Petrie?"

"Come with me, I want to point out something."

Tempe followed the slim woman to the front of her house. She paused near a double set of windows on the far side of the front door. Waving her arms, Mrs. Petrie said, "That's my kitchen. I was fixing a salad for a luncheon I'm attending at the women's club tomorrow when I noticed a light at the Fitzgeralds'."

She pointed directly across the road at another large home perched atop another hill, and continued, "Gene and Ruthann are on vacation."

"Perhaps they came home early," Tempe suggested.

"That's what I thought at first and almost gave them a call, but there was something strange about the light. It seemed to be moving around. I stepped outside to see better, and that's exactly what was happening. The light was moving like someone inside was walking around with a flashlight." She grabbed Tempe's arm and lowered her voice, "I bet it's a burglar. I told them they ought to get an alarm."

"I'll go over and check it out."

"Do you think you ought to do that by yourself?"

"I'll be fine. Can you tell me how the Fitzgeralds' house is laid out?"

While Tempe kept an eye on the structure across the way, Mrs. Petrie described the interior of her neighbor's home.

"Do they have a dog?"

"Oh, yes. A little Sheltie, but they can't be parted from him. They took him along on their trip."

Tempe paused at the Blazer long enough to report to the dispatcher and ask for backup but left her vehicle parked in Petries' driveway. No need to warn the intruder she was on her way. Though she shouldn't search alone it would take at least twenty minutes for back-up to arrive and it was possible whoever was inside the house had spotted her vehicle and might escape.

Staying close to the ornamental shrubs lining the curving drive, Tempe hurried toward the house. She skirted around the corner, heading for the large patio in the back. The yard was dark except for the pool lights causing shimmering blue-green reflections against the white exterior wall. Sliding along the wall, Tempe came to the first group of windows and peeked inside. Though unlit, she could make out the cabinets and appliances in a large kitchen. The door was locked.

The drapes were tightly closed on the next window, but from Mrs. Petrie's description it should open to the dining room. Next was the family room, and a sliding glass door. Tempe pushed on it until it gave. She slid it slowly, stopping when it opened enough for her to slip inside.

Standing quietly, Tempe listened. She could hear voices coming from another part of the house—sounded like a television. Perhaps she was in luck and whoever it was had didn't know she'd been called. No need to rush.

She unsnapped her holster and took out her gun. She had no idea what she might run into. When her eyes adjusted to the darkness, she found herself surrounded by lots of furniture, including a pool table and bar. The floor was covered with a thick carpet that muffled her footsteps. She moved slowly around the edges of the room until she reached a door that was slightly ajar. Proceeding cautiously, she poked her head around and peeked inside. It was the dining room. No one was there. She continued around the perimeter of the family room, carefully avoiding furniture, anything that might make a noise.

When she reached a large double door, she pushed her shoulder against it. It creaked loudly. She pulled back, gun held in both hands, and listened. When she heard nothing, she wrapped herself around the opening until she could slip into the hall. Glancing quickly one way and then the other, Tempe saw nothing threatening, but there was no cover. Keeping her back to the hall, she sidestepped quickly toward the sound of the television.

She slid past several closed doors. When she reached the last door, it stood slightly ajar, a ray of light spilling out onto the carpeted floor.

Peeking through the small opening, Tempe spotted the bottom of a large bed, with a flowered peach-and-pale-green spread. She could also see legs, from about the calf down, encased in drab green camouflage trousers and combat boots. Ronnie.

Holding her revolver firmly in both hands, Tempe banged the door open and stepped into the room. "Stay where you are, Keplinger," she ordered.

As he flung himself off the other side of the bed, Tempe caught a glimpse of a gun.

"Don't be foolish, Ronnie. Drop your weapon."

Tempe heard scrambling noises. Ronnie leaped to his feet, gun in hand.

There was no cover, nothing to jump behind. "I don't want to shoot you, Ronnie. Put the gun down."

He continued to lift it slowly.

Pointing at his ankles, Tempe said, "If you don't drop the gun right this second, I'm shooting."

Obviously Ronnie sensed she meant what she said, and dropped his weapon.

"Put your hands on top of your head." She stepped around the bed and kicked his gun out of reach.

After holstering her own revolver, she quickly patted him down.

"Get on the floor and put your hands behind your back."

"Aw, Deputy, you don't have to cuff me," Ronnie whined.

"Oh, yes I do, Ronnie. You've proven I can't trust you."

"I didn't want to go to jail."

"Too bad. Now you'll be charged with resisting arrest and threatening an officer of the law, as well as breaking-and-entering."

"I wouldn't have shot you. You know that."

"It certainly looked like that's what you were planning to do."

After she had him cuffed, she radioed in. As she learned backup was on its way, she heard a siren way off in the distance. "Come on, Ronnie, let's go outside."

As she pushed him ahead of her, he glanced back over his shoulder. "I'm not a criminal. I didn't steal nothing."

"You broke into the house, that's enough."

"Didn't break in," he muttered. "The sliding door wasn't locked."

Ignoring his comment, she asked, "What was that you were going to tell me about your mother's murder?"

"You don't expect me to tell you now, do you?"

She nudged him along. "There isn't anything to tell is there, Ronnie?"

His shoulders drooped lower as he moved slowly ahead of her.

"What about the anonymous letter and the threatening phone calls left on my answering machine, Ronnie? What was that all about?"

He stopped suddenly and she almost ran into him.

"I don't know what you're talking about." He sounded truly shocked by her question, and though he'd certainly lied to her previously, she believed him.

"Keep moving." If it hadn't been Ronnie, who could it be? It was time to start treating those phone threats seriously.

❦

The process of booking Ronnie and writing reports took the remainder of Tempe's shift.

Again the blinking red light of the answering machine greeted her upon her entrance into her house.

Blair was home and asleep. His VW was in the driveway and though his beeper always awakened him, the telephone ringing in the kitchen or the master bedroom never did.

The only message was from the same menacing, disguised voice speaking a single sentence. "It won't be long now."

A shiver of fear skittered up Tempe's spine.

Chapter 15

Tempe heard the familiar grind of Hutch's old truck pulling into the driveway. She ran to greet him. "You're home early."

He embraced her. "I missed you."

After a long kiss, he held her at arms' length. "You look wonderful. How are things?"

"As usual, it has been busy around here. How was the conference?"

He grabbed his suitcase from the truck's cab. Arms around each other, they entered the house. "I learned a lot, met a bunch of interesting people, but I'm glad to be home."

"Hungry?" Tempe asked.

"Nope, had breakfast on the road. However, I could use another cup of coffee."

"Coming right up."

While she poured the coffee, Hutch enthusiastically gave her the highlights of the conference. She sat across from him, sipping from a mug as she listened.

When he'd finished, he asked, "How was my substitute?"

"I'm afraid I don't know. We've had some excitement since you've been gone."

"Oh, well, I'm sure the church members will fill me in. Tell me what's happened."

She quickly summarized the events of the last couple of days, downplaying her last confrontation with Ronnie. She finished with, "So Ronnie and Spence are both in jail."

"Spence ought to know better. As for Ronnie, when he's released he's going to need some help. Perhaps I can do something for him."

"That would be good, but he may be in there for a while."

"So what are your plans for today?"

"I hope you won't mind, but I feel like I ought to visit Tom's girlfriend. "

"Ah, yes, Annie Johnson. Why do you want to see her?"

Tempe didn't want to tell Hutch about the continuing phone threats. Tom was the only suspect left if the person making the threatening phone calls was the killer. Ronnie and Spence were in jail when the last call was made. There was another reason to check on Annie.

"I'd like to find out how she's doing. Tom was abusive with Jackie. I want to make sure he isn't acting the same way toward Annie."

"Probably a good idea, though I'm not sure she'll be honest with you about something like that."

"But I can warn her about him."

"She probably won't appreciate it."

"I know, but I have to do something."

He leaned over the table to kiss her. "You care so much, that's one of the reasons I'm so crazy about you."

Tempe thought of caring as a flaw. She was expected to be helpful in all situations but never allow her emotions to enter in. An impossible requirement.

Before she could comment, the phone rang. Hutch answered and handed it to her. "For you. I'm going to unpack."

"Thought you ought to know," Sergeant Guthrie said, "Gullott's wife bailed him out and Keplinger has been taken over to the county jail."

She wasn't surprised by either bit of information.

Hutch had church business, but they made plans to be together for dinner and an evening at home.

Annie lived in a large log cabin-style home surrounded by pines and cedars on the edge of the national forest. Though obviously surprised, she greeted Tempe with genuine warmth. "For goodness sake, how nice to see you. Do come in. What brings you to this neck of the woods?" She opened the door wide, and motioned Tempe inside.

The first floor was a huge room with a big rock fireplace at one end, several uncovered windows framed the spectacular view, the kitchen separated only by a polished wood bar. A circular staircase with open risers wound its way to the rooms above.

"Actually, I'm just visiting." Tempe said.

"I wondered, since you aren't in uniform."

"Your appearance is so different that it's rather disconcerting," Tempe confessed.

Annie giggled. "To tell the truth, I'm still surprised when I look at myself in the mirror."

Tempe could see the remnants of the younger, though much plainer Annie Kruziek when she smiled, despite her surgically altered pert nose, aquamarine contacts, false eyelashes, and collagen-swollen upper lip.

"Oh, goodness, what am I thinking. Please, have a seat. Would you like something to drink? Coffee? I always have a pot going for Tom. I never know when he might pop in."

"No, thanks, Annie." Tempe sat on one end of a butterscotch-colored leather couch.

Annie smiled again. She perched expectantly on the plump cushion of the matching arm chair, her bosom threatening to explode from the scooped neckline of her teal-green blouse.

"This is a lovely house," Tempe said.

"I love it. Of course my husband, bless his soul, had it built just for me. I picked out the furniture." She beamed and fluffed her bright red curls.

"Everything is beautiful." Tempe glanced approvingly at the many western paintings on the walls, and the western artifacts grouped among the pastel pottery on the rough-hewn but obviously expensive tables. A collection of antique and modern handguns, rifles and shotguns was arranged above and on either side of the fireplace in several glass cases.

"That's an impressive display of firearms," Tempe said.

"They all work," Annie said. "Preston ... my first husband ... taught me how to clean and shoot each one."

It was time to get to the reasons for the visit. "I was certainly surprised to see you at Jackie Cannata's funeral."

"Remember. We were friends at school."

No, Tempe didn't. "I only remember you and Yvette palling around."

"We did for a while. But Jackie and I were friends later. I didn't really think I ought to go to the services with Tom, since we've been seeing each other, but he insisted. Said people might as well get used to our being together."

"How long have you been a couple?" Tempe asked.

Annie picked at one of her long, painted nails. "I'm kind of embarrassed to tell you."

"I already know it was before Jackie died."

"She and Tom didn't get along. I didn't have anything to do with that," Annie said.

"I wanted to talk to you about Tom and Jackie's relationship."

"Tom pretty much filled me in on that."

"Did he tell you that he physically abused his wife?"

A shadow crossed Annie's face briefly before her bright smile returned. "What I know is she had a drinking problem. Tom complained about it a lot. She'd quit being a real wife to him years ago."

"You've only heard his side of it, Annie. I saw what he did to her just before her death. She had to have stitches. Did he tell you that?"

She straightened her back and nodded. "Yes, he did. And Jackie did most of that to herself."

"That's not true, Annie."

She held her head high. "It doesn't matter, Tempe. I love Tom."

"Did you know that Tom's car was seen parked outside his house the night Jackie was killed?"

Annie's face turned crimson. "That's not true! He was here with me that night!"

Before Tempe could question her further, the front door banged open and Tom stormed in. "What's the matter? Has something happened here?" Glowering, he glanced from Tempe to Annie.

Tempe got to her feet. "Nothing's wrong, Tom. I happened to be driving by and decided to visit Annie. We're old friends from school you know."

"If you're so chummy, why haven't you stopped by before?" he snarled. Turning to Annie, he asked in a much nicer voice, "What's been going on? She been pumping you about me?"

Annie jumped up and went to Tom, tucking her arm in his. "It wasn't anything like that, sweetie. I've been showing off the house, that's all."

"It's truly lovely, Annie, but I better be heading on home." Tempe moved toward the door.

Tom glared at her for a moment, before lifting his head. "Got some news you can pass on to that nut-case, Gullott. Tell him I'm draining the pond. That ought to make him happy."

"I'm sure it will. What made you decide to do that?" She was sure it wasn't for Spence's benefit.

"All this yakking about my pond got the building inspector on my ass. I didn't take out any permits, didn't think I had to. I knew what I was doing. But it doesn't matter, I'm putting the property on the market."

"You've always got a home here with me, sweetie," Annie cooed.

"Yeah." Tom didn't look all that happy about the prospect.

Driving home, Tempe paid little attention to the scenery around her, something she usually enjoyed. The road was already crowded with campers and motor homes heading out of the mountains on an early start home. But the slow-moving traffic didn't bother her. She was thinking about her visit with Annie.

Again she had an intense and unexpected flash of recollection. A teenager again, she hurried through the high school quad on the way to eat in the cafeteria. Jackie and her group wearing their "Ditto" jeans, tube tops, and fancy vests, converged on pudgy Yvette and plain Annie. "You ought to quit hanging around with Yvette, Annie. Why don't you come out on the front lawn with us?" Jackie said. It was an unwritten rule that only members of the most popular groups ate lunch on the lawn. Tempe had wondered about Jackie's interest in Annie.

Yvette's lower lip quavered and her eyes were moist. "Why are you so mean to me?"

"Because you're a nothing."

Tempe remembered her mixed feelings at the time: partly relief because they weren't picking on her but also a deep sadness because she knew the pain of that kind of rejection. She'd put all that behind her long ago. Strange how it was all becoming so vivid again.

❧❧

Tempe spent the afternoon grocery shopping and preparing a special dinner in honor of Hutch's homecoming. He arrived as she finished setting the table. She'd gathered a bouquet of lupine and poppies from the backyard and arranged them in a vase in the center of the tablecloth.

After kissing her, he lifted the lid from the pot on the stove and sniffed. "Yum. Smells wonderful. What do you call this?"

"Cioppini."

Blair burst in the door, took in the flowers and the best dishes and raised a blond eyebrow. "What's the occasion?"

"Celebrating Hutch's return." Tempe beamed at her husband.

"Did you have a good time?" Blair asked.

"Yes, but it's always good to be home. How was your weekend, son?"

"Exciting and busy. Holiday weekends usually are."

"Dinner's ready," she said. "Wash your hands, and we'll bring each other up-to-date while we're eating."

The seafood and vegetable stew was delicious and the conversation lively. Hutch offered anecdotes about his conference and fellow attendees, and what he'd already heard from some of the church members about his substitute's sermon. He also said that Clare Brody, though not completely recovered, had been allowed to go home. He'd stopped by to see her.

Blair gave a descriptive rundown on the many calls he'd gone on over the long weekend. Tempe was amazed at how her son could talk and eat at the same. He managed to wolf down two huge helpings of the Cioppinni, along with three pieces of sourdough bread, and still finished long before either his mother or Hutch.

"That was super, Mom. If you'll excuse me, I'm going to take a shower. I promised I'd go back to the fire station for a couple of hours this evening."

When he'd gone, Hutch asked, "How'd your visit go with Annie?"

"Not as well as I hoped. Tom arrived before we could finish our conversation."

"Did you tell her about his treatment of Jackie?"

"Oh, yes, but he'd already made up excuses and denied it all. Of course she's going to believe him."

"Not surprising."

"She also told me that he was at her house the night Jackie was murdered."

"Giving him an alibi after all."

"Except for the fact that Yvette said she saw his BMW parked in the driveway for a short time."

"What do you think?"

"I don't really know what to think."

Hutch reached across the table and took her hand in his. "Have you had more threatening phone calls?"

She hadn't planned to tell him about them, but since he asked, she decided to be truthful. "Afraid so. I thought Ronnie was responsible, but he acted genuinely surprised when I asked him, and said he hadn't made the calls. But he hasn't been particularly honest with me about anything else. I got another call after he and Gullott were arrested, but I'm not sure that lets them out. After all, I don't really know when the call came in. Frankly, I have no idea who's doing it."

"I suppose it could be Tom, though it doesn't sound like something he would do. I'd expect him to be more out in the open if he was going to do any threatening."

"My feeling exactly." She thought for a moment. "One thing I hadn't considered before is whether or not it's a coincidence that the calls always come in when I'm not here to answer them."

"Wouldn't it have to be? After all, how would someone know whether or not you were home? Unless, of course ... "

Tempe finished his sentence. "Whoever it is, is following me."

Hutch frowned, worry apparent in his gray eyes. "Gracious, Tempe, I hope that's not so. Do you have any reason to believe that might be true?"

"I hadn't even considered it before so I haven't been paying attention. It's a possibility, I suppose." She had another flash of memory. "Oh, my."

"What?" Hutch gripped her fingers tightly.

"Saturday night, after I left Ronnie in that abandoned house, I saw a car without its lights on make a U-turn and speed off. I would have gone after it, but that's when I was called to assist the highway patrol with Spence. I forgot about that until now."

"I want you to tell Sergeant Guthrie about this."

"What am I going to say? I don't know that anyone's following me. I don't even know what kind of car I saw. It was too dark. The sergeant will think I'm paranoid."

"Better that he thinks that than have someone harm you."

"What could he do, sweetheart? If it's true that someone is following me, I'll have to find out who it is."

"I don't like the sound of this."

"Don't worry. I'll be careful." She squeezed his hand before pulling hers from his grasp. "After I clean up the kitchen, I'm challenging you to a game of backgammon."

Hutch pulled her into his arms. "I can't help but worry. I love you so much, I couldn't bear to have something happen to you."

She smoothed his ruffled hair from his brow. "Nothing's going to happen to me, sweetheart."

Hutch helped with the dishes, but before they got to the backgammon game, the phone rang.

Chapter 16

Tempe answered the phone in her usual manner, "This is Deputy Crabtree."

It was a dispatcher from the substation. "Sorry to bother you on your night off, Deputy, but Sergeant Guthrie said you should go on this call."

"What is it?" Tempe asked, picking up a pen.

Hutch frowned.

"We've had a 911 from a Mr. McKimson. Says there's a disturbance across the street from him, some sort of altercation between two men."

"Did the caller say who the men were?"

"No, he didn't identify them, he just wants us to send a deputy right away before someone gets hurt."

Tempe told Hutch what she knew about the situation. "I have no choice. I have to go."

"You aren't wearing your uniform," he protested.

"I don't have time to change." She tucked her blouse into her slacks. "The duty deputy is being sent too, so I'll have back up. It'll be okay."

Frowning, Hutch asked, "Who do you think is fighting?"

"I have no idea. Maybe Spence and Tom again, though I can't imagine why Tom would be there. Probably something to do with the pond even though he told me he was draining it."

❧❧

It was still light though the sun had disappeared behind the hills when Tempe turned into the Deerfield cul-de-sac.

A red Suburban was parked in front of the LaRue home. Emory La Rue and Spence Gullott danced around in the middle of the front yard, their fists balled and held high in front of them. Hovering near her open front door, Yvette hugged herself fearfully.

"Oh brother," Tempe breathed as she pulled the Blazer into the La Rue driveway.

Throwing open the driver's door, she jumped out hollering, "What's the trouble here?"

Yvette skirted around the sparring men, moving toward Tempe. "Oh, Tempe, thank goodness you're here. Spence has gone berserk! I think he wants to kill my husband."

Tempe thought that was impossible. Though certainly much shorter and out of shape, Emory seemed to know a lot more about defending himself than Spence did about attacking. The tall, gaunt man flailed and punched, but Emory blocked each blow with one of his big forearms.

"Cut it out, Gullott." Emory ducked one of his opponent's higher thrusts.

"Stop this instant!" Tempe shouted like a mother trying to end a skirmish between schoolboys.

"This idiot started it. I'll be glad to stop if he'll quit swinging." Emory stepped back from his opponent.

"Don't you call me an idiot, you big hunk of blubber!" Gullott threw one last punch and lost his balance, collapsing onto the grass. His glasses hung crazily from one ear.

"Stay right where you are, Spence," Tempe ordered.

Gasping for breath, Emory doubled over, placing his hands on his knees.

"Are you all right?" Yvette put a chubby arm around her husband.

"Which one of you is going to tell me what this is all about?" Tempe positioned herself near Gullott.

Her arm still around her husband, Yvette began. "Spence appeared on our doorstep about twenty minutes ago. Needless to say, we were surprised to see him. Without a fare-thee-well or a how-do-you-do, he started raving at me. I have no idea what he was talking about."

Emory straightened himself. "That skinny coward shoved my wife. That's when I got involved. I pushed him away from the door and then he started hollering and yelling. Wasn't making any sense. I told him to get the hell out of here, and that's when he started swinging on me."

Tempe wondered what had happened to her promised back-up.

No siren could be heard coming up the highway.

"You know perfectly well what I came here for." Gullott sounded winded as he maneuvered himself to a sitting position, and adjusted his glasses.

"No, I don't," Emory said.

"Well, your wife does."

Yvette shrugged and raised her eyebrows.

"Why don't you tell us what the problem is?" Tempe suggested. "Perhaps together we can work it out in a sensible manner."

"Can I get up?" Gullott asked.

"If you'll behave," Tempe said.

Awkwardly, Gullott got to his feet. "Actually, I'm glad you're here, Deputy. This has something to do with you too."

"Oh, really?"

"Remember when you asked me how I knew Jackie Cannata had been shot before it was public knowledge?"

"Yes, I remember." Tempe wondered where this was going.

"For a while I didn't know just where I'd heard. And I know you were wondering if I had something to do with Jackie's death. I don't know how you could even think such a thing. Mad as I've been at Tom about the pond, I would never killed him or his wife. I'm not a violent man." He moved his arms away from his sides, palms out.

"Ha! Couldn't prove it by me," Emory said.

"For a nonviolent person, you've certainly been behaving in a violent manner," Tempe said.

Gullott's long face turned purple. He took a deep breath and exhaled. "I haven't been myself lately."

"Whatever that is," Emory muttered.

Gullott glared at Emory.

Tempe warned, "Let's not have any more of that, Mr. LaRue. Now go on, Spence, tell us what brought you over here tonight."

"I've been racking my brain trying to figure out who told me that Jackie Cannata had been shot. Finally it came to me. It was her." Gullott pointed a long, knobby finger at Yvette.

"Why, I never did any such thing." Yvette clung to her husband's arm.

"Oh yes she did," Gullott shook his extended finger. "And that's why I came over here, to get Yvette to tell you she was the one who told me."

Yvette rolled her eyes, and put a plump finger to her lips. "Oh, dear. Maybe I did."

"And when did you find out?" Tempe asked.

"I was right here that night when they brought Jackie's body out of the house, don't you know?" Yvette pursed her lips. "I saw the hole in her chest. Wasn't too hard to figure out she'd been shot. I didn't realize it was a secret or I wouldn't have told anyone."

Yvette had been close enough, Tempe supposed. Might even have heard her conversation with the fireman. And she definitely wasn't the type to keep anything to herself.

Turning to Spence, Tempe said, "It would have been more sensible if you'd explained all this to Yvette and Emory, especially after all the trouble you've been in lately."

"That was precisely why I came over here, to straighten this matter out. And I did tell Yvette what I wanted. She started yelling at me and then her husband jumped in."

"I had no idea what you were talking about, Spence. You were talking so fast I couldn't make heads or tails of it. When I told you I didn't want to talk to you, you shoved me. Of course my husband jumped to my defense." Yvette sounded sympathetic.

"I suspect this was a communication problem," Tempe said. "Let this be a lesson to you, Spence. Take a little more time explaining yourself. Make sure people really understand what you're after before you lose your temper."

"Yeah ... well ... I thought I was making myself clear." He swiped at the lank forelock hanging in his eyes. "Guess I didn't. Sorry, Emory, Yvette. It won't happen again, I promise." All bluster and bravado deserted Gullott, leaving him crushed and deflated.

"Apology accepted." Yvette smiled and nudged her husband. "Emory?"

"Okay. Just don't pull anything like this again. Come on, Yvette, let's go inside. All this exercise made me hungry."

Yvette gazed at Tempe. "Is it okay?"

"Certainly."

Yvette followed her husband but kept glancing curiously back at Tempe and Spence Gullott until her husband closed their front door.

Tempe turned her attention to Gullott. "I want you to promise me that you'll leave the LaRues alone from now on, do you understand?"

He nodded.

"Have you heard the news about the pond?"

His chin snapped upward. "What news is that?"

"Tom is draining his pond. It might already be empty."

"Oh."

"Is that all you have to say? I thought you'd be thrilled."

"Can I go home?" Gullott looked sick. "I don't feel good."

Tempe nodded. That wasn't the reaction she expected from him. "Sure, you can go."

After he drove off, Tempe decided to check out the pond.

Leaving the Blazer in the LaRues' driveway, she headed across the street toward the burned-out remains of the Cannatas' home. Tempe felt a pull of sadness for the way Jackie's life ended along with a twinge of guilt for not being present to protect her. No matter that Tempe had a good excuse, she would always feel bad because she should have been there.

A large, redwood deck jutted out from the burned ruins of the back of the house, the only visible damages were ugly black scorch marks and a scattering of ash. What was left reeked of damp smoke. An untended flower garden was already overrun by weeds. Tall willows and full cottonwoods surrounded the site of the pond.

Tempe walked across the yard, through a gate in a chain link fence and followed a path that meandered through tall grasses and around boulders until she reached the pond. It was an enormous, gaping crater with a small puddle in the bottom. No wonder Spence had been so upset. That was a huge volume of water looming above his home. It was surprising that he hadn't reacted more positively to the news about it being drained.

As she stood on the edge, staring at the slick, muddy sides, she spotted an unusual protruding object. About half way down was something that looked like the barrel of a revolver.

"Oh boy." Before she had time to think about what she ought to do, she heard someone calling.

"Hey, Crabtree."

She turned to see the handsome Deputy Bradley heading toward her. Her back-up had finally arrived.

"What'cha doing?"

She'd forgotten to call in the resolution of the fight between Emory and Spence to the dispatcher. "Hey, Bradley. I've got something to show you." Since he was on duty and she wasn't, he could take care of what she'd found.

"Sorry I took so long, I was out by the reservation clearing up an accident. Where's the big fight?" Bradley stopped beside her.

"Oh, they kissed and made up and went home. Take a look at that."

Frowning, Bradley said, "Looks like one hell of a big mud hole."

"It's that all right, but look where I'm pointing."

He squinted. "Oh ... is that a gun?"

"Bet it's the one used by Jackie Cannata's killer."

"You're probably right. Which one of us is gonna get it?"

"Not me. I'm not on duty," Tempe said.

"Terrific." Bradley rolled his eyes.

"If I were you, I wouldn't do anything until you've reported what you've found."

"You were the one who spotted it," Bradley said.

"I don't mind if you take the credit," Tempe said, backing away quickly.

"Hey, wait a minute."

Tempe waved a hand at him, as she trotted toward the burned shell of the house. Hutch would be proud of her. There was still time for their backgammon game.

⁊ ⁊

"You're home early." Hutch smiled as he slipped a piece of paper between the pages of the book he'd been reading. "Come sit here." He patted the cushion on the couch. "Can I get you anything?"

"Nope. But there's still time for me to beat you at backgammon." She'd brought the leather case from the kitchen, and held it out to him.

"Ah ha, pretty confident, aren't you?"

"I'm feeling real lucky."

"What brought this on?" Hutch took the case from her and opened it on the coffee table.

"I stopped the fight between Spence and Emory before it got serious." She plopped down beside him.

He gaped at her for a moment. "Spence and Emory? For goodness sake, what would they have to fight about?"

"Emory was protecting his wife." Tempe explained what had gone on. "But the most exciting thing that happened is I think I found the murder weapon."

"Hey, that's terrific. Where was it?"

"I took a look at Tom's pond, which is nearly empty now. I spotted a gun stuck in the mud about halfway down the side but I left it there for Deputy Bradley to worry about." She giggled. "He wasn't too happy when I took off."

"I'm surprised you didn't stay."

"Are you kidding? I wasn't about to hang around until the detectives decided what to do about the gun. They might want to come see it for themselves. I certainly didn't want to climb into that muddy mess to get it. Bradley can handle that all by himself."

"But I'm sure you want to know who the gun belongs to."

"I already know. It'll be registered to Tom. But they won't find out anything positive about it until tomorrow."

"Won't they be able to get fingerprints?"

"That's doubtful. Despite what you see on television, it's almost impossible to get any prints off a revolver grip."

"Doesn't this prove it was Tom who shot his wife?" Hutch asked.

"Not necessarily. It only proves that it was his gun that did the job. Anyone who came into that room could have grabbed that gun. It's unlikely he'd have tossed it into his own pond, and I doubt that he would have drained the pond so willingly if he'd disposed of it there."

"So who does that leave?"

"There's always Ronnie."

"I know you don't believe he did it."

Tempe considered the options for a moment. "Maybe Spence. He's certainly been acting strangely. When I told him Tom had drained the pond, he said he was sick. He could hardly wait to get away from me."

"But why would he kill Jackie?"

"If he did, it was a mistake."

"How could he make a mistake like that?"

"I don't know." She reached for the dice container. "Let's play backgammon. Are you ready for defeat?"

CHAPTER 17

Tempe and Hutch enjoyed a leisurely breakfast before he left to make pastoral calls. He said he planned to use some of the techniques he'd learned at the conference, and he was anxious to see how they worked. His excitement tickled Tempe.

She expected, and hoped, that her day would be boring and ordinary as she tackled much needed housework. Immersing herself in chores, Tempe kept pushing away unwanted thoughts about Jackie's murder and all those involved with it.

For lunch, she ate a bowl of tomato soup and began considering what she might fix for dinner. Spaghetti sounded good.

Tempe had begun to rejoice in having a complete day off when the sergeant called.

"I knew it was too good to be true," she said.

"What?"

She laughed. "I was merely thinking that, for a change, I might have an entire day off."

"If you don't want to hear about the gun you found yesterday, or the arson investigator's report, that's fine with me. I merely called as a favor."

"Don't hang up. Of course I want to hear."

Tempe detected amusement in his voice as he continued, "More tests are underway, but as of now it looks like the bullet that killed Jackie came from the gun you found in the pond. The gun is registered to Tom Cannata."

"That's what I expected."

"The last word on the fire is that it was started by an accelerant, most likely gasoline, poured on the kitchen floor."

"All interesting, but none of it really helps point out who the killer is, does it?"

"Morrison says his money is still on the kid, but Richards is lean-ing toward Cannata. Says he's the only one with a motive."

"Tom's alibi is shaky. It hinges on his girlfriend's word. After all, there was an eyewitness that put him at the scene at the right time."

"Sounds good to me."

"Except for one thing. Why would he drain the pond if he was the one who tossed the gun there? It really doesn't make sense."

"Maybe he thought he could get back there and find it before anyone else did."

"I don't know, Sergeant. Doesn't sound reasonable to me."

"Murderers are seldom reasonable."

Tempe sighed. After all she'd done to keep from thinking about the murder, here it was, back in a rush. "Tell the detectives not to forget about Spence Gullott." She described what had happened the night before.

"I'll tell them, but I don't think they rate him high on their list of suspects."

"What's going to happen with Ronnie Keplinger?" she asked.

"He's been arraigned and bail set."

"No one's going to put up bail for him. Poor kid."

"You amaze me, Crabtree. You're the one who arrested Keplinger."

"I can't help feeling sorry for him, Sergeant. He doesn't have any-one who cares about him."

"For crying out loud, you sound like a bleeding heart."

"I've known Ronnie since he was a little boy, and my son is the same age."

"You can't save 'em all, Crabtree."

"I know." But she wished she could do something for Ronnie.

After the phone call, Tempe poked around in the refrigerator and cupboards to check on what she needed for the spaghetti. Determined not to dwell on the murder, she headed for the market in town to pick up salad greens, and fresh mushrooms for the sauce.

As she entered the store, she ran into Annie. She wore tight blue jeans, another low-cut tank-top, and high-heeled cowboy boots. Smil-ing a greeting, Tempe started to pass by, but Annie grabbed her arm.

"I want to apologize for the way Tom acted when you were over. No one realizes how hard all this has been on him. After all, it was his wife who was killed. Even if he didn't love her anymore, he does have feelings."

Tempe didn't think Jackie's death or the manner in which she died bothered Tom at all, but there was no point in arguing. All she wanted to do was make her purchases and return home, but Annie clung to her.

"There's something else." She lowered her false eyelashes for a moment, and shook out her mane of bright red curls. "I have a confession to make."

Oh, dear. What now?

Annie glanced around. The people lined up at the two cash registers were staring at them. "Why don't we go outside?"

"I really need to do some shopping," Tempe said.

"This will only take a minute."

Sighing, Tempe followed her. Outside, they stepped to the corner of the building, away from the front doors.

"What is it, Annie?" Tempe wondered if she really wanted to hear what Annie had to say.

"You'll probably think I'm silly for letting this bother me so much but I can't get it out of my head. I've just felt so guilty ever since I heard about Jackie's murder."

"What have you got to feel guilty about, Annie?"

"You have no idea how much I enjoyed the fact that Jackie's husband preferred me to her." She lifted her chin, and Tempe could see the pride in Annie's face.

"Why?" Tempe asked.

"You remember how Jackie always lorded it over all of us when we were in school. She acted like she was better than everyone else."

Tempe did remember, but what came back at that moment was Annie and Jackie walking arm-and-arm down a high school corridor. "I thought you and Jackie were buddies."

"Jackie used me, just like she did all her friends. I was too dumb to realize it until it was too late."

"That was a long time ago, Annie."

"I suppose, but it seems like yesterday." Her eyes glazed for a moment. The red curls rippled as she shook her head again. "I've never been able to forget how Jackie made me feel. One minute she was buttering me up when she wanted me to do something for her, and the next she acted like I was invisible."

Invisible was better than having insults hurled at you and being the brunt of jokes like what had happened to Tempe and Yvette. A flood of humiliation left from a long ago time surprised Tempe.

"Quit dwelling on it, Annie. Jackie's dead. She can't hurt you anymore."

"It's because she's dead that I feel guilty because Tom loves me and not her."

Tempe put her hand on Annie's shoulder. "I can't do anything for you. You probably should get professional help." She thought about suggesting Hutch but decided against it. "I really do have to go now."

"One more thing you ought to know." Annie paused.

"What's that?"

"Tom's talking about bailing Ronnie out of jail."

Tempe was shocked. "Why on earth would he do that?"

"Ronnie called him. I couldn't hear what he said, of course, and Tom didn't tell me. But he did say, 'Might be better for me if the kid was free.' What do you think he meant, Tempe?"

"I have no idea." But she did have a hunch that it had something to do with the fact that both Tom and Ronnie were suspects. "Think seriously about getting some counseling, Annie."

Maybe she needed some too. She still felt the residue of that rush of humiliation and wished she could talk to Hutch, but he wouldn't be home until supper time. She had no way of knowing where to find him. But she did know who she could talk to right away—Doretha.

❦

After making the spaghetti sauce and leaving it simmering in a crock-pot, Tempe called Doretha who hadn't been the least bit surprised to hear from Tempe. They immediately agreed to meet.

Wearing a simple denim dress, her silver hair pulled back into its usual bun, Doretha welcomed Tempe at the door. Doretha led her through the living room and outside to the back yard. A redwood picnic table held a variety of dried plants and grasses, and a basket in progress.

"Do you mind if I work while we visit?" She seated herself on a bench and picked up a tool that appeared to have been made from an animal bone. Using her fingers and the awl, Doretha began working on the basket.

"That's beautiful." Tempe admired the complex design evolving beneath the shaman's fingertips. "What is all this?"

"Sticks and plants I collected and dried." She identified each one as she pointed to them. "See the pine needles? That's red bud, and willow, sour berry and thistle, wild oats, and basket grass."

Tempe sat on a leather stool at the end of the table where Doretha worked. "Who are you making this for?"

"Perhaps a gift. I enjoy making baskets. It makes me think of the women who came before us. They used baskets for many purposes. Big ones for back packs to carry supplies and wood, smaller ones for gathering berries and acorns. Some were for sifting and others for cooking. Today we weave baskets to keep the skill alive, and to remind us of our heritage. But enough about that. You sounded urgent on the phone. Why are you here?"

Tempe could hear the river, though she couldn't see it from where they sat. Sunlight filtered through the protective overhang of the oaks, dappling the table and patio. Hummingbirds darted overhead, dipping their beaks into feeders fastened to the thick limbs of the nearby trees.

"I'm remembering things from my school days, things I'd forgotten," Tempe began.

"Things that aren't pleasant." Doretha dipped the awl into the basket, tugging and pulling on the thin dried grass as she wove it through and around the thicker, horizontal ribs.

"Not pleasant at all. But I don't understand why they're coming back with such clarity. They have nothing to do with my life today."

"Are you sure? Tell me about them."

"Jackie Cannata is part of these memories. I suppose her murder is what is dredging all this up again."

"No doubt. What is it exactly you remember?"

"It wasn't an enjoyable time. I don't even like to think about it."

Doretha poked at the dried materials and picked another length of reed that her fingers quickly tucking and weaving it into the growing basket. "Tell me what you remember. If you face it squarely, it will be less painful."

Tempe inhaled deeply, smelling the pungent odors from the herb garden, the sweetness of the wild flowers beginning to bloom among the rocks, and the faint scent from the river. It was difficult to dredge up pain while sitting in such a nurturing place, but that was why she was there.

"I grew up in Bear Creek. Along with everyone else, I had a great childhood. I didn't think I was different from any of the other kids. Oh, I knew my grandma was an Indian, but she was just my grandma. I loved her and she loved me. I sat on her lap for hours while she told me stories about the old days." Tempe could feel her grandmother's lap and the softness of her bosom as she rested her head against it.

"My grandmother died when I was eleven. Unfortunately, I hardly remember her stories."

"What a shame."

"Frankly, I've found it much easier to live in the present than to reminisce about the past."

"But the past can teach us much about how to live today."

"My grandmother's death was just the beginning of my pain. In high school I was tormented because of my mixed blood. My parents died in a car wreck soon after I graduated, and my first husband was killed."

"Everything that happens to us becomes a part of who we are. You've experienced growth from each of those events."

"No doubt, but I don't like to dwell on them."

"Of course not." Doretha's fingers continued to work, selecting each length of dried grass or plant, weaving and tucking them with the bone awl. "The universe is made up of good and evil forces. At the same time they are benevolent or dangerous. Because I felt you were in danger, I invited you to participate in the starlight ceremony to heighten your senses, to make you more aware of what was going on around you. These flashes of memories you've been having are a part of this awareness. Instead of pushing them away, you should be studying them."

"I don't see how all that ugly stuff from high school could possibly have any relevance now," Tempe said.

"Why are you fighting it? You just told me it had something to do with the murdered woman. Is there anyone else in your life today that is entwined in the memory flashes you are having?"

"Yes. Annie is living with Jackie Cannata's husband, Tom. In fact, I had a brief conversation with her this morning. It seems she feels guilty, not because of her affair with Tom, but because of the delight she experienced in taking Tom away from Jackie."

"Why is that?"

"I remember Annie and Jackie as friends, but Annie said Jackie used her. In what way, I'm not sure. I wasn't comfortable with the conversation, but It seems kind of strange she'd get so much satisfaction out of getting back at Jackie after all these years."

"Unless she let the wound fester. Everyone handles pain differently, some dwell on it, others bury it like you have. Tell me about Jackie."

A picture of Jackie lying dead on the front lawn of her burning house came immediately to Tempe's mind. But that wasn't the Jackie Doretha wanted to hear about.

"Jackie was the leader of the most popular clique. She always wore the latest hairdos and fashions. But she was mean. She enjoyed poking fun at people, calling them names, causing others to laugh at them. I was the brunt of her cruelty many times. Her name for me was 'Halfbreed.' I didn't even know what that meant at first, just that it was demeaning because all her friends giggled when she called me that."

Tempe remembered the first time, how she'd cried and run into the bathroom. She stared at herself in the mirror, trying to see what it was that made everyone laugh. Her black hair was brushed neatly around her shoulders, her round face with its high cheekbones and golden complexion looked the same as it did every day.

Finally it dawned on her that it was the Native American blood that she inherited from her grandmother that seemed to offend them, something she was unable to change. How she'd wished she could dye her hair and alter her bone structure. Anything to be more like the other girls. Staying out of Jackie's way was all she could do.

"Were they mean to anyone else like that?"

"Of course, anyone they looked down on, which was everyone outside their group." Saying that, Tempe knew she meant someone that was not only in her past but also in her present, like Yvette.

"I can tell by your expression you've thought of someone else."

Tempe nodded. "Yvette LaRue. She was a Slader back then."

The emerging pattern on the side of the basket grew more distinct as Doretha wove in darker brown grass. "Tell me about her."

"Yvette was always pudgy and rather plain. I remember Jackie making fun of her weight. To be perfectly honest, I didn't feel sorry for her. I was just glad someone else was the brunt of Jackie's meanness.

Yvette and Annie were inseparable for a long time, but then Annie started to hang around with Jackie's group."

"Wasn't that unusual? What do you think happened?"

"I'm not really sure, though I have a hunch it was merely another way for Jackie to hurt Yvette."

"What kind of relationship did Jackie and Yvette have as adults?"

"The interesting part is that they were neighbors. Yvette and her husband live in one of the homes in the same cul-de-sac as the Cannatas. Jackie didn't like Yvette much, thought she was a snoop. But Yvette wanted to be friends."

"Doesn't that seem strange considering their adversarial relationship as teenagers?" Doretha asked.

"I hadn't really thought about it. Like I told you, I've repressed all those painful memories from my high school days."

"Maybe you ought to think about them in more depth. You might learn something about Yvette and Jackie, and perhaps, even yourself."

"One important fact you don't know is that Yvette is the one who called 911 when Tom was physically abusing Jackie."

Doretha glanced up from her work. She brushed a silver strand away from her eyes. "Interesting. How did she act around Jackie?"

"Like she wanted to be her friend."

"And Jackie? Was she still mean to her?"

"She certainly didn't want Yvette for a buddy, that was obvious, but she was polite enough. She had enough problems of her own, an abusive husband and strange acting son."

"I think all the answers lie in the past," Doretha held up her handiwork to examine it. The basket was nearly complete.

"The answers to what? Who murdered Jackie?"

"The answers to your questions, whatever they may be."

CHAPTER 18

"My favorite." Hutch lifted the lid of the crock pot and inhaled. "You make the best spaghetti."

Tempe grinned. "That's what you say about everything I cook. Is that a hint to get me to cook more often?"

He circled her waist with his arms and pulled her close. "Nope, just letting you know I appreciate it when you do." He kissed her. "How was your day?"

"Great. Believe it or not, except for a phone call from the Sergeant, this has really been a day off."

"Don't speak too soon. It isn't over yet." He nibbled her ear.

"Are you ready to eat, or is something else on your mind?" she asked.

"Actually, I'm starved but I'll take a rain check for the 'something else'." He released her and began setting the table. "Is Blair going to be here?"

"No, he's in town. Something to do with graduation plans."

"Does that mean we'll have the evening to ourselves?"

"Some of it, anyway. How was your day? Did your new techniques work as well as you hoped?"

While Tempe put the water on for the noodles and began making a salad, Hutch told her about his successful visitations ending with, "The proof will be in how many new faces we see in church on Sunday."

"I don't see how anyone could possibly resist you."

While they ate, Tempe said, "I ran into Annie at the store. She said that Tom is planning to put up bail for Ronnie. Surprising, don't you think?"

"Perhaps Tom is turning over a new leaf." Hutch twirled some noodles on his fork.

"I find that hard to believe."

He shook his head. "You're so cynical."

"My job makes me that way."

"This sauce is wonderful. Your best ever."

"I also did some visiting today."

"Really? Who'd you see?"

"Doretha."

A shadow crossed Hutch's face but it disappeared quickly. He smiled. "How is she doing? Did she get a new car yet?"

"I didn't think to ask. She was making a basket. Fascinating to watch her."

"Is that why you went all the way out there, to watch her make a basket?"

"No, of course not. I wanted to talk to her."

"What about?"

"Something I'd like to run by you too." She didn't plan to tell him about the starlight ceremony, but she did want to hear his take on what she and Doretha discussed.

"Of course," Hutch said.

"Remember I told you I was having memory flashes about my high school days?"

He nodded and forked more of the noodles and sauce into his mouth.

"What I've been remembering isn't pleasant, but Jackie and Annie and Yvette LaRue are part of it. It isn't something I've thought about for years, in fact, I haven't wanted to."

"So why is it all coming back to you now?"

"Doretha's explanation was, 'All the answers lie in the past.'"

"I think Doretha is right. They probably do."

"You're as bad as she is. The answers to what?"

Hutch wiped his mouth. "The answers to whatever you're seeking."

"What am I seeking? The only thing I can think of that has any connection to Jackie, Annie, and Yvette is, 'who killed Jackie?' Now what could my memories about the three of them and me too, have to do with the murder?"

"Seems to me that's something you're going to have to spend time reflecting on."

"Thanks a lot." He wasn't any more helpful than Doretha.

"After all, sweetheart, they are your memories. You are the only one who can figure out their significance."

"You don't realize how difficult that is. I don't want to think about those days, especially not the part about Jackie. She was so mean. Not just to me, but anyone she considered an outsider. She picked on the fat kids, the ones with bad complexions, anyone who wore shabby or unfashionable clothes, and of course me, because I looked different."

"She was jealous because you were so beautiful," Hutch said.

"I'm positive that thought never entered her head."

Tempe reached across the table and caressed Hutch's freckled cheek. "I love you."

"I love you too."

"Yes, my darling, I know. You're always so wonderful to me."

"Of course, I am." He frowned as though he didn't quite understand. "Would it help you to talk about those days? Maybe putting your feelings into words will help you isolate whatever it is that you need to know. Not only that, Tempe, it could be good to get all those old emotions out into the open."

"I haven't even thought about any of this stuff for years. I put it all behind me. It has nothing to do with my life now."

"Obviously it does or these memories wouldn't be popping up."

"Is it because Jackie, Annie, and Yvette have come into my life again?"

"No doubt."

Tempe concentrated on her spaghetti for a moment. Was it worth it to bring back all those disturbing memories? Would she really learn anything that could help her today? How could reliving a time when she was shunned by her peers because of her ancestry help solve anything in her life today?

She remembered one time going into the girl's restroom as Yvette was coming out. Surprisingly, Yvette had a huge smile on her round face. "Hi, Tempe, guess what?"

Without waiting for comment, she continued on. "I'm running for Garconettes. Someone put my name in for it, and once you're nominated it's a sure thing you'll get in." She bubbled with excitement. Garconettes was a school service club. There was another club that the more popular girls belonged to, but being a member of Garconettes was a possibility for the rest. Membership was gained through nomination and votes of other members.

"Hey, that's great."

Yvette gave her a quick hug. "Wish me luck. This is the best thing that ever happened to me."

Tempe had never wanted to belong to any of the clubs and was surprised Yvette did. It was much simpler to concentrate on the school work and stay out of everyone's way.

"You've just remembered something else." Hutch brought Tempe back to the present.

"Yes, but like all the rest, it has no relevance to anything."

"Run it by me."

She described the brief encounter she'd had with Yvette so long ago.

"Well, did she get in the club?" Hutch asked.

"I have no idea," Tempe said. "The only thing Yvette and I had in common was the fact that we were both picked on by Jackie. We didn't hang around together. She lived in Dennison and I lived here in Bear Creek. After school I rode the bus home and didn't see any of the Dennison kids."

"All of this will come together eventually, I'm sure."

Tempe shook her head. "I certainly can't make any sense of it yet."

The phone rang.

"Oh, no," Hutch said.

Tempe picked up the receiver. "Deputy Crabtree."

It was Sergeant Guthrie. "Have a bit of news thought you needed to know. Ronnie Keplinger made bail."

After hanging up, Tempe said, "Tom did it. He bailed Ronnie out of jail."

"What does that mean?"

"No doubt Ronnie's back in Bear Creek. Since the bail was high, Tom's going to be keeping an eye on him. Probably even got him a place to stay."

"Maybe he's at Annie's."

"Oh, I can't imagine that but I could be wrong. I never thought Tom would help Ronnie. I'll have to find out where he is."

"Not tonight, I hope."

"No, not tonight." She grinned at him. "Why don't I take you up on that 'rain check?' The dishes will wait."

∽❧

The next morning, Tempe phoned Annie and learned that Tom had paid for a room for Ronnie at Bear Creek Inn. Though she would have liked to have gone there to talk to Ronnie, she agreed instead to go shopping in Dennison with Hutch. There would be plenty of time for a chat with Ronnie later.

Ronnie was on Hutch's mind too. "I wonder if I could find some-one at the church who would be willing to give Ronnie a job." He drove out of the mountains, past the lake, and the many orange groves.

"That may be difficult since he is eventually going to have to stand trial and spend time in jail."

"But if he were living a more productive life the judge might be more lenient, isn't that so?"

"Perhaps. But he's going to have to make some other changes too, beginning with the way he looks."

"One step at a time, sweetheart, one step at a time." He concen-trated on the road ahead. Tempe knew his mind was busy making plans for Ronnie's rehabilitation. Obviously he had accepted her be-lief that Ronnie didn't kill his mother.

∽❧

No sooner was Tempe in the Blazer and on duty than she spotted Tom opening the door of his BMW parked in front of the Inn. She made a U-turn and pulled in behind him.

He glowered as she approached. "What the heck do you want now?"

"Heard you bailed Ronnie out of jail."

"Yep. What's it to you?"

"Curious, that's all."

"Isn't any of your business, but I suppose you'll be bugging me until you find out." He smiled, displaying his big, white teeth. "Got to feeling sorry for the kid. Didn't have a chance with a mother like Jackie." He glanced down for a moment. "Guess I didn't help matters any."

Could he possibly be feeling some compassion for his step-son? Tempe found it hard to believe. Tom Cannata wasn't the type to be magnanimous, least of all to a stepson whom he barely tolerated. More likely, he was putting on an act.

"Have you been visiting him? Annie told me you got him a room here at the Inn? How's he doing?"

The smile disappeared briefly but returned. "Stopped by to give him some money."

"Have you thought about offering him a job? He's going to need something productive to do while he's waiting for trial."

Tom's face transformed, his tan darkened, and his eyes turned cold. "I've done enough for the stupid bastard. Bailing him out, getting him a place to stay. He can damn well find his own job."

"That isn't going to be easy, you know."

"Not my problem." He slid into the driver seat, slammed the door and started the BMW.

"Nice talking to you," Tempe said to his exhaust.

Great way to start the evening. Climbing back into the Blazer, she thought about the encounter. Neither charity nor kindness had prompted Tom to bail his stepson out of jail. If he were the murderer, he might want Ronnie out to confuse things. She couldn't help wondering even though it wasn't her problem.

She made her usual loop down to the lake, cruising through the nearly empty campgrounds, back to town and on into the mountains. Traffic was light, and the radio quiet.

About a mile before the national forest boundary where she planned to turn around, she received a "Shots fired" call.

Gun shots weren't usually cause for alarm in Bear Creek. Most residents owned guns. Some knew how to use them; some didn't. The common use was to eradicate pests like rattlesnakes, ground squirrels, and an occasional marauding mountain lion, or coyote. Folks liked to target practice, and usually no one paid much attention.

But the general location of the complaint was close to Annie Johnson's house and Tempe felt a stab of foreboding.

CHAPTER 19

A silver BMW flew toward Tempe's Blazer and whizzed past, going in the opposite direction.

"Oh, oh, there goes Tom." Tempe reached for her microphone and reported the location of the speeding vehicle, issuing a warning that the driver might be armed and dangerous.

Switching on her emergency lights and pressing the accelerator, Tempe sped toward Annie's, dreading what she might find.

All the lights seemed to be on in the two-story log cabin as Tempe braked to a stop close to the front deck. A figure was silhouetted in the doorway as she started up the steps at a run.

Thank God. It was Annie. She held a fancy. silver-plated revolver in her hand, and lowered it to her side. "I thought you were Tom."

"What's going on here? Were you shooting that thing?"

Grinning, Annie held up the revolver. "Sure was. This is a Merwin, Hulbert and Company revolver. Made in the 1870's,.44-40 caliber. My husband was mighty proud of it."

Upon closer observation, Tempe could see small rubies embedded in the engraving on the grip. It was one of the guns she'd noticed on display in a case in Annie's front room.

"I saw Tom speeding away from here. Were you shooting at him?" Tempe asked.

"Darn tooting!"

"You didn't hit him, I hope."

"Nope. Though I would have if I had to. I wanted him out of here." She glanced down the road. "Come on inside, Tempe, Don't mind the mess." Annie led the way.

A butterscotch colored chair rested on its side, both bar stools lay on the floor, several pictures hung cockeyed, and a lamp was broken. The scene reminded Tempe of when she had been called to the

Cannatas' house the first time. "Oh, my, you and Tom really had a problem," Tempe said.

Annie put the gun on the bar that divided the kitchen from the living room. "I don't suppose you'd want a drink. That's what I need right now."

"I wouldn't mind some coffee." Tempe righted the bar stools and perched on one.

Annie poured Tempe a cup of coffee, and half glass of Jack Daniels for herself. She took a big swallow. "You were absolutely right about Tom. If I'd been honest with myself, I'd have realized it before tonight. I've been so lonely since my husband died, and Tom seemed to be the answer." She took another sip. "Like I told you, I got this perverse satisfaction from stealing Jackie's husband. Now I know he wasn't worth the effort."

"Tell me what happened tonight," Tempe said, warming her hands on the mug.

"According to Tom, he ran into you after going to see Ronnie."

"That's right. Not a particularly friendly encounter."

"He came home and began giving me hell for 'blabbing to the pig' as he put it. We argued for a while then he began knocking over the furniture. When I told him to stop it, he pushed me."

She took another long drink and began to laugh. "Something snapped inside me. I told him I wouldn't put up with that kind of treatment from him."

"He made this ugly face ... guess it was supposed to scare me ... and told me he'd treat me anyway he damned well pleased. That was it! I grabbed the gun off the wall and told him to get out. He laughed and said, 'That stupid gun isn't even loaded.' But I looked him square in the eye and took aim. 'You haven't got the guts,' he said. 'Course he didn't think I meant business, but I changed his mind when I fired over his head. He took notice, but he still didn't do much more than back up a few feet. When I fired the second time, and I knew he heard the bullet whistle right over his head, he hightailed it out the front door."

Tempe couldn't help laughing at the scene Annie described.

"I got off one more shot as he was climbing into his precious BMW." Annie giggled. "Honestly, Tempe, I don't know what I ever saw in that man."

Tempe didn't know either. "I want you to be careful, Annie. You probably haven't heard the last of him. You know there's always the possibility he killed Jackie."

"Don't you worry one little bit about me. I wouldn't hesitate to put a bullet into Mr. Tom Cannata if need be. But I don't think there'll be a problem. You should have seen his face, he was scared to death. He won't be coming around here again." She drained her glass. "I feel better already."

"Tomorrow I want you to go to town and get a restraining order against Tom."

Annie patted the revolver. "This is all the restraining order I need."

"For crying out loud, Annie, I don't want you to shoot him."

"Oh, don't worry, I won't, unless it's absolutely necessary."

Tempe took a last sip of coffee and stood. "Okay. But do be careful."

Coming around the bar, her face animated, Annie said, "I have a great idea. Tomorrow I'm going to the Inn and ask Ronnie if he wants to move in with me. I've got plenty of room, and I wouldn't be so lonely with him around. Give me someone to take care of. The couple of times I've seen him, we got along real well. We've gone through a lot of the same stuff. I think I might be able to help him."

"Ronnie has lots of problems, Annie, that might not be such a good idea."

"I think it's down right splendid. Won't it bug the heck out of Tom?"

⁂

While making her rounds later that evening, Tempe had the creepy feeling that someone was following her, but she didn't spot any vehicle that stayed behind her for any length of time.

She enjoyed an uninterrupted dinner break with Hutch and Blair.

"What are your plans for this evening?" Tempe asked.

After taking a sip of his coffee, Hutch said, "I'm having Bible study at the church later."

Between bites Blair said, "I'm going to a refresher CPR and First Aid course at the fire station."

After returning to work, Tempe learned that Tom had been ticketed for speeding soon after leaving Annie's. Though she kept an eye out for him, she didn't spot his BMW.

When she stopped by the house for a potty break, neither her husband nor Blair had returned. She was greeted by the message light blinking on the answering machine.

She punched the PLAY button, and started for the hall, stopping abruptly when she recognized the guttural, disguised voice.

"Come to the abandoned house tonight at midnight or you'll be sorry."

There were two or three abandoned houses in and around Bear Creek, but Tempe knew that the mysterious caller meant the one where Ronnie had been hiding. If she was right, the caller was Ronnie.

Though she knew she ought to report her destination to the dispatcher, she felt she'd rather decide what to do after she'd talked to Ronnie. But as soon as she climbed into the Blazer and headed toward the old house, the creepy feeling she had earlier returned with intensity.

She glanced in her rear view mirror often but spotted no headlights that remained with her for any length of time. Approaching the abandoned house, deep shadows from the trees and dense underbrush on both sides of the road increased the menace Tempe felt. The structure was completely dark.

Tempe drove down the road a ways before turning around and coming back to park. No other vehicles were visible.

Though it certainly appeared that no one was here, Tempe felt she was walking into a trap. "If I had good sense, I wouldn't go in." Even as she spoke, she slid out of the Blazer. She closed the door quietly, knowing that if Ronnie waited inside, he was already aware she'd arrived. Playing the flashlight beam along the overgrown path, she headed toward the porch. The closer she got, the more she felt the profound threat of impending peril.

The first step creaked loudly. She paused and listened. An owl hooted three times. She could hear the traffic on the highway. A cow bawled. No sound came from inside the house.

The rotten boards of the porch groaned as she walked to the door. It stood ajar. The interior was so black Tempe saw nothing until she shined her flashlight inside.

"Hey, Ronnie," she hollered. "It's me, Deputy Crabtree. What is it you want?"

There was no answer. He wanted to play games. She put her back against the door jamb and slid around it until she was inside. Listening, she waited until her eyes adjusted somewhat to the darkness.

Maybe he changed his mind and wasn't here after all. She couldn't think of any reason why he would lie in wait for her or even want to talk to her, for that matter.

"Ronnie," she called again. Still no answer.

If it wasn't Ronnie who demanded the meeting, who could it be? Maybe Tom, but lurking in an empty house wasn't his style.

Tempe moved around the edge of the room until she reached the door to the hall. It led only to blackness. Sighing, she shined her flashlight ahead and started down the hall. Stopping at each door, she swept her beam through the empty rooms.

Common sense told her no one was there. Her uneasiness increased to a discomforting alarm. When she finally reached the back bedroom where Ronnie had stayed previously, she cautiously moved inside, shining the flashlight in all four corners of the room. Except for the trash and the dangling cobwebs, the room was empty.

This was a wild goose chase. Whoever made the threatening calls was playing games with her. Shaking her head in an attempt to dispel the menace that continued to surround her, Tempe headed back down the hall toward the front of the house.

Before she reached the living room, the front door slammed shut with a loud bang.

CHAPTER 20

Unless the wind had suddenly risen, which wasn't likely, Tempe was no longer alone in the house. "Who's there? Ronnie, is that you?"

The emotion that had dogged her since she came inside swelled. She sensed an ominous presence. She paused, and she heard Doretha's voice inside her head. "Be cautious."

Mustering her courage, she unsnapped the holster on her right side and gripped her flashlight in her left hand as she willed herself to take the remaining few steps that would bring her to the living room.

What was the strong odor? She sniffed and immediately identified gasoline.

She swept the flashlight beam from wall to wall. The light caught the round, pale face of Yvette LaRue. Her small eyes bulged and sparked above the pudgy cheeks. Her plump body was swathed in dark clothing.

"Yvette. For goodness sake, what are you doing here?" Tempe asked.

"Turn off the flashlight," Yvette ordered as she flicked open a cigarette lighter. A tiny gold and blue blaze turned her face into a shadowed masque of madness.

Tempe chose to comply until she knew what was on the woman's mind.

Yvette continued. "You know exactly why I'm here. You're the only one who could possibly connect me with Jackie's death. I don't want to kill you, but you forced me to because of all your prying. You wouldn't pay any attention to my warnings. I knew that eventually you would figure it out. I'm going to get rid of you the same way I did her."

In Yvette's other hand, she held a torch wrapped in rags. She touched the lighter to it. A burst of flames threw grotesque shadows on the walls.

"I don't know what you're talking about, Yvette." Tempe realized the gasoline she smelled had been poured over the floor, and knew the situation was worse than she thought.

Yvette cackled. "Oh, I think you do. After all, you're the only one who knew how much I hated Jackie."

"Frankly, Yvette, I had no idea how you felt about her." Tempe's hand hovered near her holster.

"Playing dumb isn't going to change anything. In a few seconds I'm dropping the torch and this old house will go up in flames. You're going to die in this fire, Tempe. No one will ever know I was here." The flickering blaze distorted Yvette's features even more.

"Jackie tormented me in high school too, Yvette," Tempe said, hoping to distract her. "But I never wanted to kill her."

"She stole my best friend, Annie."

"Jackie was mean to Annie too."

"The worst was when she ruined my chances to join the Garconettes. Jackie told the other members to vote against me. Annie said so."

"All that happened years ago, back when we were teenagers. I don't see how it can possibly matter now."

"It matters because Jackie was treating me the same way again. It took me years to get over what she did to me, and to finally gain confidence in myself. I even spent time in an institution. I married the first man who asked me. Emory has been good to me, but it certainly isn't the kind of marriage I dreamed about."

Obviously Yvette blamed Jackie for everything that happened in her life.

"I tried to be friends with Jackie, give her a chance to make up for what she did before. But she brushed me aside. Then I was asked to join Bear Creek Women's Club. When I found out Jackie belonged, I went to her house and pleaded with her not to vote against me, but she laughed at me. I knew she was going to ruin my chances of becoming a member. I had to stop her."

Jackie probably didn't have a clue what Yvette was talking about. Tempe doubted that Jackie even thought about Yvette from her high school days. "That's why you killed her? Because of a club?"

Yvette ignored Tempe. "I couldn't bear to go through all that misery again. I wasn't going to let her hurt me any more." She brushed away a tear. "Enough. It's time I took care of what I came for."

Keeping her voice calm, Tempe said, "Tell me how you killed Jackie." She hoped to keep Yvette talking until she decided how to overpower her.

"It was easy. I watched the house and saw Ronnie come out. He didn't lock the door. I just walked in. I went upstairs. All the things she did to me came back in a rush. She pretended she didn't know what I was talking about.

"There was a gun on her night stand. I grabbed it and shot her. I put the gun in my pocket. I ran home and got a can of gasoline out of our garage. It was easy to splash it all over the kitchen floor and set it on fire. I threw the gun in the pond and went back home to wait for all the excitement."

She waved the torch, a spark fell to the floor. "If you'd kept your nose out of other people's business, you wouldn't be in this fix now."

Yvette tossed the torch in her direction, and Tempe threw herself toward Yvette, butting her in the stomach and sending her smashing against the wall.

Fire exploded all around them.

～⁂～

Hutch couldn't sleep. He'd been lying awake for nearly an hour and felt something was wrong. Several times he got up and wandered through the house. He'd gazed out the window hoping to see Tempe's Blazer pulling into the driveway. Clouds hid the moon.

He'd heard Blair come in earlier. He tried to pray, but he couldn't concentrate. Ideas about what might have happened to Tempe kept popping into his mind.

Finally, he couldn't stand it any longer and dressed. He paused outside Blair's room. Probably he was asleep, but he might know something. Hutch knocked. No answer. He knocked again, louder. "Blair, are you awake?"

A sleepy "Huh?" came from within.

Hutch pounded even harder. "Wake up, Blair. I need to talk to you."

"Yeah, what's wrong?" The bed squeaked.

Blair opened his door. He wore baggy shorts, his chest was bare, his blond hair ruffled. He yawned. "What's going on?"

"Have you heard anything from your mother?"

"No, should I?" He scratched his head, blinked his eyes, and became alert. "Has something happened?"

"That's what I'm wondering. I'm worried about her."

"You know Mom won't let me listen to my scanner at night. She thinks I'll get up and go on a call." He rolled his eyes. "I'll turn it on now and see if anything's going on."

"Good idea." The phone rang. "I'll get that."

Hutch dashed down the hall toward the kitchen. He snatched up the receiver. "Tempe?"

"No, it's Doretha Nightwalker."

Hutch didn't know whether to feel relieved or irritated. He glanced at his watch, it was after twelve.

"Yes, Doretha, what can I do for you?"

"I'd like to speak to Tempe."

"She hasn't come in from work yet."

"I don't want to alarm you, but I believe Tempe's in grave danger."

"I'm having those same feelings."

Blair galloped down the hall, pulling a T-shirt over his head, untied tennis shoes flopping on his feet. "There's a fire at an abandoned house not far from here."

"We'll take the truck," Hutch said, and into the phone, "Thanks for calling, Doretha. We're going to look for Tempe now." He hung up.

They hurried outside. Hutch backed the truck out of the yard and headed down the road. He sniffed the night air. "Smell that?"

"Yeah. Smoke. Can you go faster?"

Hutch pushed the accelerator to the floor and gripped the steering wheel.

"I couldn't bear it if anything happened to your mother."

Beside him, Blair took a deep breath. "I'm glad she married you."

"I love her so much."

"I love her too. She's been so much happier with you around. Man, I hope she's all right."

"Me too, son, me too." Hutch reached over and squeezed Blair's shoulder. "Where is that house anyway?"

"Around the next corner." Blair leaned forward, peering through the windshield.

Smoke billowed from the abandoned structure. Tempe's Blazer was parked beside the road. Another vehicle was behind it.

"Whose car is that?" Hutch asked. "Do you recognize it?"

"Looks familiar. Belongs to someone in Bear Creek."

Hutch parked and jumped out of the truck. "I'm going after your mom."

⁓⁓

Though Tempe had taken Yvette by surprise, the woman recovered quickly. She kicked and flailed at Tempe. "Let go of me."

"Come on, Yvette, we have to get out of here." Tempe scrambled to her feet and grabbed Yvette's plump wrist. "Get up."

The fire crackled and snapped behind Tempe. She felt the blistering heat at her back. Smoke burned her eyes and made it difficult to breathe. "We don't have much time." Tempe dodged Yvette's kicks and maneuvered her around until she faced the door. "Let's get out of here."

"I'm not going to jail." She planted her feet firmly on the floor seeming not to notice the flames licking around her. "Jackie deserved to die."

"I'm not leaving you here." Using both hands, Tempe used all her strength trying to maneuver Yvette outside.

Sirens wailed. Squealing brakes and pounding footsteps distracted Tempe for an instant.

Yvette yanked her arm from Tempe's grasp, scrambled upright and darted into the wall of fire.

"Oh, dear God! Come back, Yvette!" With her hands in front of her face, Tempe bent over intending to go after Yvette, but strong arms grasped her around the waist and pulled her out onto the porch.

"No, no, I have to get Yvette." She struggled to free herself until she realized it was Hutch who held her. She allowed him to pull her away. "Someone has to save her."

"Leave that up to the firefighters," Hutch said.

Flames exploded, pouring from doors and windows. Hutch led Tempe back toward the Blazer. Two fire trucks arrived, along with several other vehicles. Men and women dressed in turn-out gear, helmets, jackets, trousers, and boots, pulled equipment and hoses from the truck. Tempe spotted Blair. Orders were shouted as everyone dashed about, occupied with the frenzied mechanics of fighting the inferno.

"Anybody inside?" the Captain asked.

Tempe quickly explained about Yvette.

In minutes, water was sprayed on the fire with little effect.

"Oh, Hutch, Yvette doesn't have a chance," Tempe said.

"I don't think she wants one."

For a long while they stared at the flames consuming the building. Tempe leaned against Hutch and thought about Yvette. Though they'd never been friends, they had experienced the same pain, though each had handled it differently. Tempe had buried the hurts and thought she'd forgotten them while Yvette nursed hers and kept them festering until her hatred had driven her to madness and murder.

When the firemen finally seemed to be winning their battle, Tempe turned to Hutch. "Thank you for coming to my rescue, but what brought you here?"

"I couldn't sleep. I had this horrible feeling that something was wrong. And I wasn't the only one. Doretha called to warn that you were in danger."

"You were both right."

"About you being in danger? That was rather obvious when I got here and found you grappling with Yvette inside that inferno."

"I meant that you both told me the answer was in the past. If I'd been more objective, I might have suspected Yvette killed Jackie."

"Ronnie and Tom were much more obvious suspects."

"And Spence Gullott added to the confusion." She thought about the other suspects for a moment. Ronnie would have to spend some time in jail, but if he took Annie up on her offer, he would have a place to live. No doubt Hutch would help him find a job and counsel him about leading a productive life. As for Tom, he'd bear watching. Hopefully, Spence would calm down now that the pond was drained, and return to his more normal, eccentric self.

Of course it would fall to Tempe to bring the dreadful news about Yvette to her husband, certainly not one of the best aspects of her job. Explaining all this to the detectives would be another difficult chore, but one that could wait until morning.

One thing she had learned, from now on she'd pay closer attention to her instincts.

As the fire died down, Blair joined them, giving Tempe a hug. "I'm so glad you're okay, Mom."

"Thanks, honey."

After a long silence, Tempe asked, "Wasn't it strange that you and Doretha had the same feeling at the same time?"

Hutch shook his head. "No, I'm beginning to realize it wasn't strange at all."

They stood for a long time, mother, son, husband, with arms around each other, staring at the smoke rising from the ruins of the smoldering house.

The End

ABOUT THE AUTHOR

Marilyn Meredith is the author of over twenty books in several genres, but mainly mystery. She embraced electronic publishing before anyone knew much about it.

She teaches writing and was an instructor for Writer's Digest School, has been a judge for several writing contest, was a founding member of the San Joaquin chapter of Sisters in Crime, serves on the board of directors of the Public Safety Writers Association, is also a member of EPIC and Mystery Writers of America.

Marilyn lives in the foothills of the Southern Sierra in California in a place much like Bear Creek where her heroine Tempe Crabtree serves as a resident deputy. She is married to the "cute sailor" she met on a blind date many years ago and is grateful for all the support he gives her and her writing career every day.

She is proud of the fact that she and her husband raised five children and now are grandparents to nineteen and great-grands to eleven.

TEMPE CRABTREE
MYSTERY SERIES

Tempe Crabtree is the resident deputy of Bear Creek, a small mountain community in the southern Sierra. Her continuing interest in the spiritual side of her heritage often causes unrest in her marriage to her minister husband.

In *Calling the Dead*, Deputy Tempe Crabtree investigates a murder that looks like death from natural causes, and a suicide that looks like murder. Putting her job on the line, she investigates the murder on her own time and without permission from her superiors. Jeopardizing her marriage, she uses Native American ways to call back the dead to learn the truth about the suicide.

Available in trade paperback and eBook from Mundania
www.Mundania.com

PIERS ANTHONY

The ChroMagic Series
Key to Chroma
Key to Destiny
Key to Havoc
Key to Liberty
Key to Survival

Of Man and Manta Series
Omnivore
Orn
OX

Macroscope

Tortoise Reform

Under a Velvet Cloak
(Incarnations of Immortality Book 8)

❧ ❧

PIERS ANTHONY & ROBERT E. MARGROFF

The Roundear Prophecy Series
Dragon's Gold
Serpent's Silver
Chimaera's Copper
Orc's Opal
Mouvar's Magic

Printed in the United States
126946LV00004B/21/A